Stirring Up Old Flames

As soon as they ordered sodas, Jake was on his feet, pulling Nancy onto the dance floor.

"This is what I really needed," Nancy said.

"The perfect way to shake away all the school blues," Jake joked, unable to take his eyes off Nancy. Right then she looked particularly beautiful—the blue of her dress matched her big eyes, and her red-blond hair glistened in the light.

After a few fast songs, the lights dimmed, and a slow tune came on. As they swayed to the rhythm of the love song, Jake felt as if he were riding the crest of a great, wonderful wave. Being this close to Nancy always gave him a heady feeling.

Jake buried his face in Nancy's hair, breathing in the clean, fresh scent of her shampoo. Suddenly he felt her body stiffen. He pulled back to look at her. She was staring toward the entrance. Jake followed her gaze.

Nancy's old boyfriend, Ned, was standing in the door, watching them dance.

NANCY DREW ON CAMPUS™

Available from ARCHWAY Paperbacks

Nancy Drew
on campus™ #16

Going Home

Carolyn Keene

AN ARCHWAY PAPERBACK
Published by POCKET BOOKS
New York London Toronto Sydney Tokyo Singapore

This book is a work of fiction. Names, characters, places and incidents are products of the author's imagination or are used fictitiously. Any resemblance to actual events or locales or persons, living or dead, is entirely coincidental.

AN ARCHWAY PAPERBACK *Original*

An Archway Paperback published by
POCKET BOOKS, a division of Simon & Schuster Inc.
1230 Avenue of the Americas, New York, NY 10020

ISBN: 0-671-56805-1

First Archway Paperback printing December 1996

10 9 8 7 6 5 4 3 2 1

Cover photos by Pat Hill Studio

Printed in the U.S.A.

IL 8+

CHAPTER 1

S chool is out! Time to party!" Nancy Drew cried to her friend George Fayne as they crossed the Wilder University campus.

"Three long, glorious days of partying," George added. The two girls joined the crowds of students streaming toward the dorms and parking lots.

Nancy pushed her thick red-blond hair back from her face and happily looked around. The atmosphere on the Wilder quad was charged and spirits were high as the campus was emptied for the long weekend break.

"I love it here." Nancy smiled. "I think Wilder feels more like home now than River Heights does. Although I *am* happy to be free of classes and studying for a few days."

"Well, in a couple of hours we'll be out of here

1

and on our way back to River Heights with our gorgeous new boyfriends," George said. "Aren't you psyched about taking Jake home?"

"It's a mixed bag," Nancy admitted. She paused to try to put her feelings into words. "I miss Dad and can't wait to see Hannah, but I have no idea how they'll react to Jake."

"How could anyone not love Jake Collins— he's brilliant, witty, and good-looking," George said.

Nancy smiled, thinking of her boyfriend's beautiful brown eyes and handsome face.

"True, but Hannah and Dad are so used to me being with Ned," Nancy continued. "I know they expected me to marry him someday." She made a face at George. "I'm sure they'll spend a lot of time comparing Jake to Ned."

"Don't sweat it, Nan. Ned was—no, *is*—terrific, but so is Jake," George said. "Don't you think your dad must have felt nervous when you first met Avery? I'm sure he was worried you might not like his girlfriend when he brought her here."

Nancy laughed with surprise. "Avery's great!" Nancy had wanted to like the first woman her dad had fallen in love with since the death of Nancy's mother years before. Fortunately, when Avery and Nancy had met, they'd become instant friends. But what if they hadn't?

"Just remember, your dad and Hannah want you to be happy. Jake's great, and they'll love him."

"I'm keeping my fingers crossed on that one."

Nancy pushed down the uneasy feeling in her stomach.

"Keep them crossed for me, too," George said with a laugh. "I'm not exactly sure how my parents are going to take to Will, either." Her face suddenly sobered. "You know, now that I think about it, I kind of wish we weren't bringing the guys home with us this weekend. I want to spend as much time with Bess as possible. I'm worried about her. Every time I've talked with her on the phone, she's sounded weird, not like herself at all."

Sadness swept over Nancy as she thought about George's cousin, Bess Marvin. Bess and her boyfriend, Paul Cody, had been in a terrible motorcycle accident a couple of weeks before. Bess's injuries weren't too serious, but Paul had been killed. Bess had gone home to River Heights to recuperate. "I agree that she's acting different," Nancy said. "And I can't wait to see her."

As they approached the Student Union, George's face lit up. "Hey, it's Kate Terrell!" she exclaimed. "Kate," George called out to her friend.

Nancy glanced up and smiled as Kate waved at them. She was standing with a good-looking guy behind a long table outside the Student Union. They were busy arranging audiocassettes on a small display shelf on one half of the table. The other half featured colorful handcrafted metal earrings.

Though the quad was crowded, no one wanted to stop long enough to check out their merchandise.

"George, Nancy, this is Jeff Rayburn," Kate said, smiling at the dark-haired guy next to her. He was small and wiry. Sunglasses hid his eyes, but his smile was warm.

"Hi," Jeff said.

"Nice earrings," Nancy said, pointing to the turquoise ones Kate was wearing.

"Thanks. Jeff sells them." Kate gazed up at Jeff. "I told him the afternoon before a long weekend isn't the hottest time for business."

Jeff shrugged off Kate's remark. "Just wait until Sunday." He turned to Nancy and George. "We're heading up to the Keelor Falls Crafts Fair. I usually sell a lot at crafts fairs and street festivals."

"Keelor Falls?" George said. "That's not far from River Heights, where we live. Nancy and I are taking Jake and Will home this weekend."

"Have you been to Keelor Falls?" Kate asked.

George nodded. "Sure, I've hiked there a lot.

"Why don't you drop by the fair on Sunday?" Jeff said. "It'll be fun. The food's great, and there's lots of live music."

"Sounds cool," George said, then glanced at Nancy. "But we're both pretty booked this weekend."

"You know, family stuff," Nancy said.

George glanced at her watch. "Oh, my gosh, I was supposed to meet Will at Jamison ten minutes ago. I gotta go." She turned. "Nice meeting you, Jeff. See ya, Kate." As George moved off toward her dorm, she yelled back over her shoulder. "Nancy, we'll hook up with you and Jake at Thayer."

"I'd better get going, too," Nancy said. "Hope you guys do great business at the crafts fair. 'Bye."

"If your plans change over the weekend," Kate called out after them, "don't forget Keelor Falls. We'll be there Sunday all day."

Kara Verbeck's sea green eyes widened at the sight of radio station KWDR's control room. Headsets hung from a wall board above a work counter that held a bewildering array of sound equipment: CD players, tape decks, two old turntables, and a control panel of some sort. Three microphones with clipboards by them were arranged on a table in front of the counter.

Kara giggled, and her friend Nikki Bennett bounced a little on her toes. "This is *so* exciting," Nikki said.

Kara couldn't agree more. She was really going to be on the radio. She was going to cohost a real talk show—something she had fantasized about ever since freshman year of high school, when she had developed a major crush on an outrageously insulting local talk-show host.

Kara, Nikki, and another girl, Montana Smith, were touring the KWDR studio with their Pi Phi sorority sister Patrice Barton, host of a popular weekly campus call-in show. Patrice had offered Montana, Kara, and Nikki a chance to host the Saturday afternoon show, and ever since, Kara couldn't concentrate on anything else.

She'd been thinking about what she would say when listeners called to discuss the latest hot topic. Kara hoped that she would come up with instant, provocative answers to whatever subject Patrice had chosen for that week's discussion.

Kara eyed the buttons and knobs warily. "What's all this stuff?" she asked under her breath.

"Montana can deal with it," Nikki answered. "Can't you, Montana?" she asked.

"Like I said, it's no sweat," Montana replied with a confident toss of her blond curls. "I'm an old hand at this."

Patrice peered at Montana over her glasses. "You did have your own radio show back in high school, right?"

"My own?" Montana repeated, looking a little surprised. "Not exactly." At the sight of Patrice's worried face, she added quickly, "But I did work on a show there. I know the ropes. Now, this is the cart for the commercials, right?" she said, pointing toward what looked like an eight-track tape. Patrice heaved a relieved sigh.

"Yes," Patrice replied. "And here's the schedule for when the commercials are to be run. They're on a short tape, with automatic cutoff like an answering machine tape. It'll rewind when it's finished. Then you just start it up again, following this cue sheet."

Montana winked at Kara and Nikki behind Patrice's back as Patrice continued her explanation.

"That's about the scoop on how to cut to the commercials and how to check the volume. And don't forget FCC regulations—you must give the station's call name and number at the top of every hour. That's really crucial. So, is everything clear?"

Kara blinked and met Patrice's serious gray eyes. Suddenly she realized she hadn't heard a word Patrice had said.

She looked at Montana. The slim blond young woman radiated confidence. Kara cleared her throat. "We'll do fine." After all, Montana knew what she was doing, Kara reminded herself.

"Don't worry, Patrice. I've got it all under control." Montana laughed. "We'll host a show Wilder won't forget!"

"So, Jake, it's *the* big weekend," said Nick Dimartini as he stopped his car for a red light on Weston's main street. Nick was giving Jake a ride from the off-campus apartment they shared to Thayer Hall, Nancy's dorm.

Jake sat in the passenger seat, his feet propped up on the dashboard. He pretended not to understand what his roommate meant. "Yeah, it'll be good to have a nice long weekend."

"Could be extra long if Nancy's dad doesn't

like you." Nick laughed as he punched Jake's shoulder.

Jake raked his fingers through his thick brown hair. Nick was too good a friend to try to fake out. "All right, I do want to make a good impression."

"Knew it," Nick said.

"Anyway, between Carson Drew and Hannah—"

"That's his girlfriend?" Nick asked.

Jake shook his head. "No, their housekeeper. She's sort of like a mother to Nancy." Jake shrugged. "But I think I'll get along with them. I do pretty well with most people."

"True."

Jake didn't want to go on talking about the meeting. He couldn't quite suppress the fear that Nancy might back off from their relationship if her dad didn't like him. Nancy and her dad were pretty close. "So, what are you doing this weekend, Dimartini?" he asked, changing the subject.

"My uncle's opening a record store in a new mall a couple of hours south of here," Nick said, turning through the main gate. "It's some town called River Heights."

"River Heights!" Jake threw back his head and laughed. "That's where Nancy lives." Jake propped his arms behind his head and grinned. "We should hook up with each other over the weekend. Will and George will be around, too."

"Sounds cool," Nick replied, "but I'm going to be pretty busy helping my uncle with the opening of the store. I promised him I'd put in as many hours as he needed me to work. But," he said as they approached Thayer Hall, "maybe some night after the store closes we can get together."

"Give me your uncle's home phone number and the name and number of the store. I'll check in with you tomorrow or Sunday, and we'll see what's up."

"Great," Nick said as he stopped in front of the dorm and Jake jumped out. "And good luck with Nancy's family!"

"Thanks," Jake said, reaching into the back-seat for his green duffel. He shouldered the bag and waved goodbye.

Jake worked his way through the crowd clogging the entrance to the Y-shaped glass-and-brick modern dorm building. He took one look at the mob waiting for the elevator. "Forget it!" he said, and tossed his duffel into a pile of bags beside the main staircase leading to the upper floors.

Whistling, he bounded up the steps two at a time toward Nancy's third-floor suite.

"What's taking Nancy so long?" George exclaimed impatiently to Will Blackfeather. "And where's Jake?" George jumped up from the sofa in the lounge of Suite 301 in Thayer Hall and checked her watch. Would Nancy ever be packed?

George glanced at Will and shook her head in dismay. "I want to get going!"

Will smoothed back his dark hair and laughed. "Calm down. What's the big hurry?"

"The sooner we get on the road, the sooner we'll be in River Heights," George said. She gestured around her. "Look at this place. It's a zoo."

"You'd think everyone was going home for semester break, instead of just a long weekend." Will's dark eyes were amused as he followed George's gaze.

Dawn Steiger's camping gear was piled in a corner near the TV, and Eileen O'Connor, another of Nancy's suitemates, was taking up half the floor of the lounge, trying to roll up drawings small enough to fit inside a plastic tube. "Can you believe I have to finish these by Tuesday at nine A.M.?" Eileen said. "I don't know why I'm even bothering to leave for the weekend."

"Because it would be too depressing to stay," Dawn tossed off as she moved her gear into the hallway. "The campus will be a ghost town."

"I'm going to see what Nancy's up to," George said. She walked down the hall to Nancy's room and poked her head in the door. Nancy's suitcase was already stuffed, and she was standing by her bed, frowning at two sweaters, one in each hand. Hearing George, she looked up.

"Which one should I take?" Nancy asked.

"Are you *still* packing?" George couldn't believe it. She started to laugh. "Nancy, it's just three days." George took one of the sweaters, tossed it in the suitcase, and began to lower the lid.

"Not yet!" Nancy stopped her. "I've still got to get my toothbrush, and I can't find my new jeans. Kara probably borrowed them again."

"By all means—add the toothbrush, while there's still room in that suitcase," George teased. She backed out of Nancy's room and straight into Casey Fontaine. The pretty redhead was pushing a small suitcase on wheels down the hall.

"Whoops!" Casey exclaimed as she collided with George. "Sorry, but if I don't get out of here in ten seconds flat, I'm going to miss my flight."

"I hear you're heading for Palm Springs," George said, walking along with her.

"Yeah, Charley and I figured this long weekend would be a good time to get together."

"I guess it's rough, spending so much time apart," George said sympathetically as they reached the elevator outside the suite. She knew Casey, a former TV star, and her actor boyfriend, Charley Stern, had recently gotten engaged.

"You can't begin to imagine. . . ." Casey said, then noticed the elevator had come. "Here's my ride. Have a good time in River Heights, George, and say hi to Bess!"

As George turned back to the suite, she saw Jake coming up the stairs. "George, is Nancy ready yet?" Jake asked as they walked into the suite.

"Not the last time I looked," George replied, "but maybe now." She noticed he didn't have a bag. "You're traveling light."

"I left my duffel bag downstairs," Jake said. "I figured I'd help Nancy carry her stuff down. Boy, it's mobbed."

"Tell me about it," George said, checking her watch again. "We should have been gone by now."

Jake stopped to talk to Will as George went back into Nancy's room.

"I'm ready," Nancy said, standing in front of the mirror and pulling a brush through her hair.

"At last," George said. "Jake's here, so we're finally going to get this act on the road."

"Ummm, is this Kara Verbeck's room?" a voice said from the doorway.

George turned around. A petite girl with short black hair was standing in the doorway. She flashed a shy, nervous smile.

"Yes. She's my roommate," Nancy replied.

"Hi, my name is Lily. Kara borrowed my jacket, and I need it back before I leave for the weekend."

Nancy rolled her eyes. "That's Kara, all right."

"It's red suede with fringe," the girl added, coming into the room.

"Hi. I'm Nancy, and this is George."

Lily nodded and quickly looked around. "Which side is Kara's?"

"Kara's closet is there," Nancy said, pointing. "I'll help you look."

I do not believe this, thought George. *We are never, ever going to get out of here.*

It seemed to take forever, but a few minutes

later Nancy emerged from Kara's closet with a red suede jacket over her arm. "Is this the one, Lily?"

Lily's face lit up. "Yes, that's it." She started out the door. "Hey, thanks, and let Kara know I took it back."

"Right!" George and Nancy said at once.

"I should leave Kara a note," Nancy said.

"It can wait," George retorted, steering Nancy out the door. "Besides, she probably won't even notice the jacket is gone in this mess."

A few minutes later George, Nancy, Will, and Jake were trooping down the stairs.

"Let's get out of here!" George cried, reaching the ground floor before anyone else.

"Wait," Jake called. "I need to get my bag." Jake rummaged through an enormous jumble of luggage at the bottom of the steps.

"Jaaaaake!" George wailed. "Hurry up. Let's get this show on the road!"

Jake grabbed a green duffel with a Wilder U logo. "Here it is."

George led the group across the crowded parking lot to Nancy's Mustang. Jake shoved the suitcases into the trunk and tossed his duffel into the backseat.

"On our way at last," Will said, jumping in the back next to George.

"Finally," George said, cuddling up next to Will. "But it's rush hour. Now it's going to take forever to get home."

"George, will you put a lid on it!" Will cried. "We're on our way."

As Nancy maneuvered the car through backed-up traffic, Will pulled George closer. She felt herself relaxing.

He murmured into her ear, "River Heights is about two hours from here, right? That gives us two hours of fun in the backseat."

George laughed softly as she lifted her face toward Will's for a kiss.

By the time Nancy hit the interstate, George was thinking maybe Will was right. Two hours on the road didn't seem very long at all.

CHAPTER 2

Ginny Yuen took the long way from the library back to Thayer Hall. In the week since she and Ray Johannson had broken up, Ginny had become an expert on campus paths that were less traveled. She didn't want to run into Ray accidentally.

"Ginny! Wait up!"

At the sound of Ray's gravelly voice, Ginny's heart sank. She took a deep breath before turning around. "Hi, Ray!" she said.

Ray stood a few feet behind her, at a bend in the path. Ginny hugged her books to her chest. Every fiber of her being yearned to rush into his arms and forget that they had broken up.

The sun glinted off Ray's dark hair. He shifted from foot to foot and looked as awkward as Ginny felt.

"Haven't seen you around for a while," Ray said with a quick, nervous smile.

"Ray." Ginny felt the color rise to her cheeks. Ever since they had decided to back away from their relationship to give each other space, Ginny hurt too much just seeing him. "Yeah, well." She lifted her eyes to meet his.

Ray searched her face, then dropped his gaze and sighed. "Mind if I walk with you a bit?"

Ginny shook her head. The few inches between them as they walked felt like a thousand miles. It took all of Ginny's willpower not to reach over and take his hand. After a few steps she asked, "So, what's new?"

Ray's smile brightened. "The Beat Poets are heading to Chicago this weekend to lay down some practice tapes at a recording studio."

"It's good you don't have to fly off to Los Angeles again," Ginny said. "It's so far, and you miss so much school." A shadow crossed Ray's face.

Ginny pursed her lips. One of the biggest issues between her and Ray had been his staying in school. He wanted to drop out and head to Los Angeles to pursue the music business. Ginny felt he should stay in school, that he needed something to fall back on in case his dreams of rock stardom didn't pan out.

"Yeah—well—I wish I *had* gone there with Spider last week. After all, it *is* my band, and I should have been in L.A. with Spider at the meeting with the Pacific Records execs about the new songs for the album. Anyway, one exec is flying in to listen to our taping session. I haven't met him yet, but Spider did when he was in Los Angeles. He said the guy is pretty cool."

"So, when are you all going?"

"Crack of dawn tomorrow. Chicago, here we come!"

Ray's enthusiasm was infectious, and Ginny couldn't help but feel happy for him. They talked a moment longer, then came to the turnoff for Thayer Hall. "Well, good luck with it," Ginny said.

"Yeah, thanks," Ray replied. He hesitated, as if he wanted to say something else. Instead, he touched her shoulder, and Ginny felt as if she were on fire. Quickly she stepped out of his reach.

Ray dropped his hand. "Have a great weekend," he said, the life draining from his voice.

"I will," Ginny mumbled, and walked away. A wave of sadness washed over her. All that talk about the band and what he was up to, but not once had Ray asked Ginny what she was doing for the weekend.

Ginny was sick at heart. She still loved Ray, but he was so involved in his own budding music career that he didn't have time to care about what was important to her.

Ginny was bursting with important things to share with someone who was more than just a friend. She had felt excited and inspired ever since she'd joined Wilder's premed volunteer program at the pediatric wing of Weston General Hospital. Ginny had fallen in love with the kids there. She was more sure every day that she wanted to be a doctor.

Ray still didn't trust that her decision to be a doctor was her own and not just that of her parents. Once it had only been *their* dream for her. After she'd met Ray and discovered she could write songs, Ginny had thought about giving up the idea of a career in medicine. Ray wanted her to have a music career with him.

But her work at the hospital had made her realize that she really did love medicine and helping people. She wasn't there to fulfill anybody else's dreams for her. This was her own decision. Ray couldn't see that, because he never listened to her. Ginny forced back the tears, realizing now that he probably never would.

"Hey, could you guys pass my duffel bag up here?" Jake said to George and Will from the front passenger seat of Nancy's car.

Nancy glanced in the rearview mirror and grinned.

George was curled up with her head on Will's lap, half-asleep. Careful not to disturb George, Will grabbed the green bag.

"Thanks," Jake said, unzipping the bag. "Whew, this is kind of heavy. I didn't think I packed that much. Hey!"

"What's wrong?" Nancy asked.

"I don't believe it. This isn't my stuff." Jake rummaged through the things in the duffel.

"What stuff?" George said sleepily. She sat up and yawned.

"I must have grabbed the wrong bag back at the dorm," Jake said, annoyed. "We were in such a rush. . . ." He turned toward George. *"You* were in such a rush!"

"Me?" George feigned innocence. "Don't blame me if you spaced out."

Jake blew out his breath.

"Do you want to go back?" Nancy suggested. "Was there something important?"

"No way!" George cried. "We're halfway home."

"She's right," Jake said. "There was nothing in my bag so important that a quick stop at a convenience store won't cure. Meanwhile, let's see if there's some ID in here, so I can call the owner. With any luck, the person will have picked up my bag and we can trade Monday night when we get back." Jake started pushing aside some clothes at the top of the bag.

"T-shirts, jeans, toothbrush. Here's a flier for some festival at Keelor Falls." Jake stopped. "Hey, these look like new tapes," he said.

"A *lot* of new tapes." Nancy whistled, glancing away from the road for a moment.

"But they're a lot of duplicates of only a few albums," Jake said. "Whoever belongs to this bag has pretty cool taste." He dug deeper into the bag and came up with a few more tapes by bands

19

currently popular with Wilder students. "Most of these cassettes are still shrink-wrapped," he said, surprised.

"Why would someone have so many unopened tapes?" Will asked.

"And so many dupes?" George remarked. "That Cybersounds title is one I've never heard of, but there have to be at least a dozen copies of it."

Nancy was quiet and thoughtful. "What was the name of Kate Terrell's friend, George?" she finally asked. "Weren't they selling tapes outside the Student Union today?"

"Yes, they were. Jeff Rayburn was his name," George said, suddenly sounding more awake. "Maybe this person's going to sell these tapes at Keelor Falls like Jeff."

"Whoever owns this bag is going to miss it, then," Nancy said. "Any luck with the ID, Jake?"

Jake searched the bag thoroughly, stacking the tapes beside him. "Nope—only this key."

Will took the key from Jake. It had a red plastic cover on the top with a number on it. "It seems to be a locker key from the Weston bus station."

"Well, the bag's owner will be looking for it," Jake said. "Meanwhile, some of these tapes are opened, so let's enjoy the music."

"Didn't you say there's one by Cybersounds?" Nancy asked. "One of your faves," she added.

"Hmmm. I don't recognize the title. Must be

a new release. I thought it wasn't going to be out for a few weeks. Anyway, it's open, so let's try it out," Jake said, popping the tape into the tape deck. A second later the car reverberated to the beat of the music.

"Being stuck with someone else's bag isn't such a downer after all," Jake said contentedly, slinging one arm around Nancy's shoulders.

Nancy reached up with one hand and twined her fingers through Jake's. "Always the optimist, Jake. That's what I love about you!"

"I can't believe it. Tomorrow we get to lay down the first tracks for our album," Spider Kelly said to Ray as they stood in front of the Beat Poets' garage rehearsal space.

Ray smiled at Spider. "You're really pumped."

"Aren't you?" Spider sounded incredulous.

"You'd better believe it," Ray said quickly. Actually, ever since he ran into Ginny, he'd been feeling pretty down. But he wasn't in the mood to talk to Spider about Ginny. "It seems like a dream, really—the contract, maybe a video, club dates, and concerts someday," he said.

Spider grinned at Ray. "Man, I can't believe how fast everything's been happening!"

"Actually, it's been happening almost *too* fast," Ray said. He ambled down the driveway toward the garage.

"In the music business, nothing can happen *too* fast," Spider remarked, unlocking the double doors to the garage. "Guess the rest of the guys aren't here yet," he said, flicking on the lights.

The place was a mess. Ray and his band had rehearsed late the night before, and the floor was littered with soda cans, pizza boxes, old newspapers. Spider pulled over a trash can and began gathering up the garbage.

Ray pitched in. He took a deep breath, savoring the familiar, slightly musty smell of the place. He loved this space.

The thought of Ginny crossed his mind, and for a moment Ray imagined he could smell the perfumed scent of her shampoo. But of course she hadn't been there in more than a week now. His spirits dropped. This was where he and Ginny had spent a lot of time writing songs together. She was so creative and gifted—her lyrics really inspired him to craft his best music.

Ray sighed audibly, then tried to shake off his melancholy by helping Spider move instruments around.

"Getting a contract sure changes everything," Spider remarked.

"The pressure's on," Ray said. "We've got to tighten our performance, and that means more hours in here."

"Or wherever . . ." Spider mused, pulling up a folding chair and straddling it. "Ray," he said earnestly, "I pretty much decided that I can't stay in school and have a music career."

Ray stretched out his legs and stared at the hole in the right knee of his jeans. "I know. It's been almost impossible to concentrate on studying." Ray felt distinctly uncomfortable even admitting that. Not that Spider would care, but Ginny would. She thought school was just as important as music. "All I really want to do is make music," he said.

"So let's do it."

Ray hesitated to say yes. He wasn't sure why. Maybe because part of him still wondered if Ginny was right—that he should get a college degree to fall back on if the music didn't pan out. Or was it because the thought of leaving Wilder and losing touch with Ginny was too hard to handle just now?

"I'm thinking about it," he finally said. "I really am. But I need to give it more time." Even to himself, Ray knew his excuse sounded pretty lame.

Spider shrugged. "Not much to think about now. We're on the brink of the big time."

Ray felt the same way. If the band's album hit the charts, Ginny would change her mind. He'd be able to show her he'd been right to follow his heart.

"By the way, Joel Hoffman phoned today."

Ray looked up quickly and frowned. "The Pacific Records guy we're hooking up with tomorrow?"

"Yeah. He wanted to talk about the session this weekend."

"Why'd he call you?" Ray asked. "I'm the leader of the band; I set up the schedules."

Spider lifted his shoulders. "Probably because I met him in Los Angeles. Maybe he felt better calling someone he already knows. No big deal, Ray."

"Uh—sure." Ray nodded slowly. "Makes sense, I guess." But the thought that Joel had bypassed him still rankled. The Beat Poets was his band. Well, when he met this Joel Hoffman dude in person, Ray would just have to show him exactly who was in charge.

"This is our block," Nancy told Jake as she turned down the street where she lived. "That's our house over there."

It was turning dark, and she and Jake had just dropped off George and Will at the Faynes'. As she turned into her driveway, Nancy felt excited and a little nervous.

She hoped her dad and Hannah liked Jake. "Home sweet home!" she said, and pulled up in front of the garage. The late-afternoon sun was sinking fast, and the light from the living room spilled out through the open curtains onto the side porch. The effect was warm and welcoming.

"Nice house," Jake said, climbing out of the car and looking around. He stretched his arms over his head and then reached for the duffel.

Nancy popped open the trunk of the car, but before she could get her suitcase out, Hannah, her father, and her father's girlfriend, Avery Fallon, poured out of the house.

Nancy hadn't expected Avery to be there.

"Nancy!" her father greeted her warmly. Carson Drew pulled Nancy into his arms, and they hugged each other hard. He leaned back, and his blue eyes searched hers. "You okay?" he asked softly. Nancy nodded and felt grateful that her father understood how difficult the past two weeks had been—Paul's death, Bess's close call . . .

"I'm fine, Dad," she replied, and pressed his hand. Then she turned around. Already Hannah had hooked her arm through Jake's.

"My, those are some cowboy boots you have on," the housekeeper remarked to Jake. Hannah grinned at Nancy in a way that made Nancy know she approved of Jake. "By the way, I'm Hannah Gruen."

Jake pumped the housekeeper's hand. "Jake Collins," he said. "So you're the one I get to quiz about Nancy's childhood." He winked at Nancy.

Hannah chuckled. "I *do* know a few funny stories. . . ."

One down, one to go, Nancy thought. Nancy unhooked Jake's arm from Hannah's and guided him toward her father. "Dad, this is Jake Collins. Jake, this is my dad. And this is Avery Fallon . . . his friend." Nancy watched her father carefully.

Carson Drew shook Jake's hand. "Good to meet you at last. We've been hearing wonderful things about you."

"Same here," Jake responded. Then Jake turned to Avery. "Good to meet you, too."

"Come on in, Jake," Avery said, beckoning him to the side door. "Hope you haven't snacked too much en route." Avery flashed Nancy a knowing smile. "Hannah's cooked an incredible dinner. You haven't lived until you've tasted her food. Right, Nan?" Avery reached out and touched Nancy's arm.

Nancy blinked. "Yes." She couldn't quite get used to the idea that Avery was there—tonight of all nights.

But she didn't have time to think much about it. A moment later they were inside the house, and everyone was talking at once.

"Why don't you bring your bag in, and I'll show you where you're sleeping," Avery said to Jake.

"I'll just leave it here by the door. It's not my bag." Jake grabbed Nancy's suitcase and explained about the bag mixup at the dorm as Nancy trailed behind them up the stairs.

At the top of the stairs, Hannah pointed out Nancy's room. The door was open, and her bedside lamp cast a warm golden glow over the simply decorated room. The sight of her room, with its blue and white wallpaper and blue chenille bedspread, made her happy. School trophies, books, and a few favorite mementos filled the bookshelves.

Jake put Nancy's suitcase at the foot of her bed and looked around, his dark eyes eagerly drinking in every detail. Nancy could tell he was trying to piece together who she was now based on who she had been when she was a little girl. But she felt a little weird when Hannah proudly pointed out the prize Nancy had won in an elementary school spelling bee. She was glad when Avery steered them into the hall.

"This is your room, Jake," Avery said, opening the door. "The bathroom's at the end of the hall."

"This is great," Jake replied, looking around the pleasantly decorated guest room. Nancy could sense that he liked it, and her family.

More importantly, she realized everyone liked Jake, too. Hannah, her father, and even Avery.

"This is going to be a terrific weekend," Jake said, curling his fingers around Nancy's as they followed the others downstairs.

"I think so," Nancy said, feeling almost totally relaxed now. Something tugged at the back of her mind, but she couldn't quite focus on it.

Everyone was getting along. What else was there to worry about? she thought as they joined her dad and Avery in the living room. If something was bugging her, she was just going to ignore it. I want everything to be perfect tonight, Nancy decided as she snuggled next to Jake on the couch.

CHAPTER 3

Bess Marvin lay on her bed, her broken right arm propped up on a pillow as she watched a woman on a TV show yell at the man she loved.

You shouldn't do that! Bess thought. You might never see him alive again. You'd never get another chance to say how much you love him.

When Bess heard the doorbell ring, she didn't even look away from the TV. A second later George's voice, then Will's, floated up to Bess's second-floor bedroom. They were talking to Bess's mother. George's voice dropped, and Bess knew she was asking how Bess was doing. She bit her lip and dug her toes deeper into the down comforter at the foot of her bed.

Bess focused on the TV show and wondered what had possessed her to say yes to Nancy's dinner invitation for that night. Jake would be there with Nancy. Will with George. They'd be with their boyfriends. And her boyfriend was . . . The thought of Paul made her insides go hollow.

"Bess?" She heard George call and then open the door.

Bess looked up. "Hi, George," she said, reluctantly aiming the remote at the set and flicking it off.

"Hi." George hung back in the doorway.

Bess smiled weakly. "I'm glad to see you." Bess meant it, but her voice sounded sort of flat.

"Me, too," George said, leaning against the door frame. "How are you? How's your arm?"

"I'm doing okay," Bess said, ruefully eyeing her cast. "My arm's better." The conversation suddenly felt forced. Bess wasn't sure what she was supposed to say next.

"And you guys?" She looked past George. "When did you get into town?"

"A couple of hours ago. Will's talking to your dad," George said. She seemed at a loss for words, too.

Bess watched as George took in the messy room. "You ready for dinner?" George glanced at the clock on the wall above Bess's bed. "I told Nancy we'd be there around seven or so. It's almost that now."

Bess nodded. "In a sec." She stood up, grabbed a brush with her left hand, and yanked it through her long blond hair. She didn't even check the mirror to see how she looked.

"Let's go," Bess said apathetically.

29

"Bess?" George stopped her at the door. "You want to talk, while we're still alone?"

"What's there to say?" Bess started down the stairs.

She heard George sigh. Bess turned around. "I'm okay. I'm feeling better." Bess pointed to the cut on her forehead. It was almost healed though still red. The black-and-blue mark on her cheek had faded considerably. "I'll be good as new soon."

"Bess, we're here for you," George said.

Beth felt a lump rise in her throat, but she forced it back. Once she started to cry, she might not stop.

"Yeah . . ." she said, lightly punching George's shoulder. "I know that. I really do." But all the friends in the world and all the love her family was showering on her couldn't change a thing.

Nothing could ever bring Paul back.

"What did I tell you, Ginny Yuen! We're not the only ones who had nowhere to go this weekend," Liz Bader exclaimed. The two roommates were headed into the Cave, the cafeteria in the basement of Rand Hall, the architecture building.

"Your instincts were right about coming here, though," Ginny told her as she looked around. With so many students gone for the weekend, the Cave wasn't crowded even though it was dinnertime. But the place had a party atmosphere. From where they were standing, Ginny could see that lots of kids were table-hopping.

"Not that I mind hanging out here this weekend," Liz said. "This is the first time since September that I'm not swamped with architecture crits."

Ginny wasn't feeling very hungry. Seeing Ray earlier had kind of killed her appetite. She grabbed a cup of tea and a sandwich and headed for the cashier.

"Hey, look who's over there," Ginny said. "Reva and Pam—I didn't think Pam would be here this weekend."

"It looks like they're saving seats for us," Liz said, pocketing her change.

"So, how are you guys doing?" Reva Ross asked, making room for Ginny as she walked up. Reva was one of Ginny and Liz's suitemates.

"My entire dorm is practically empty," Pam Miller, George's roommate in Jamison Hall, said.

"And I thought everyone in our suite but Liz and I was going away for the weekend," Reva replied.

"Stephanie's still around," Pam remarked. "I saw her at Berrigan's this afternoon when I finished work. She was starting her shift, and I think she's working an extra one tomorrow."

"What love will do for some people." Liz laughed. "Stephanie's actually become more human since Jonathan Bauer became *the* man in her life."

"I thought *I* was *the* man around here," Jamal Lewis said as he deposited his tray next to Pam's.

"Hey, hi! This is a nice surprise," Pam said.

"You are *the* man—for me—but it was Stephanie Keats's man we were talking about."

"Pam, did either you or Reva hear back from the Natural Shades company yet?" Ginny asked. She knew that Pam and Reva had entered a model contest that the cosmetics company was conducting to find young black models for their new ad campaign. Both Pam and Reva were candidates for the final selection to be announced soon.

"Nope," Pam said. "They're canvassing colleges on both coasts now. It'll be weeks until they make a decision. I think they're trying to see who can survive the waiting period."

"I, for one, might not survive," Reva said. "I'm dying of suspense."

"Speaking of suspense," Jamal interrupted, "there's a really cool blues band at the Underground tonight."

"Oh, yeah!" Pam exclaimed. "Will and George were talking about them the other day. Blue Suspense. Up-and-coming and really hot."

"Let's check 'em out!" Liz suggested.

Ginny shrank back in her seat. A band. The Underground—it was the Beat Poets' hangout. And it was her and Ray's place, where they first met. They'd shared a lot of really good times there. "I'm not in the mood," Ginny said. "You guys go."

Liz flashed Ginny a sympathetic look, before shaking her head. "Come on, Ginny, there's no reason for you not to go this weekend."

Ginny drew in her breath and thought a moment. She knew Liz was right, still. . . .

"Hey, Ginny, what's new?" The sound of Frank Chung's voice made Ginny look up. Frank was an art major who belonged to the same Asian students' association, the Asian Society, as Ginny.

"Hi, Frank," she said.

Liz reached over and pulled a chair up between her and Ginny. "Sit down."

Ginny made room for Frank and flashed him a quick smile. Frank and she had become good friends lately. It was Frank she found herself confiding in about the volunteer program at the hospital and her decision about a medical career.

"We were just thinking of heading over to the Underground," Jamal said to Frank. "Want to come?"

Frank looked at Ginny. "You going?"

Ginny hesitated. "I'm not sure."

"Come on, Ginny," Liz urged, tugging at the sleeve of Ginny's red sweater. "It'll be fun."

Ginny felt Frank's eyes on her. She began to smile. "Okay. Maybe just the first set, though," she said. "I have to work at the hospital tomorrow, the early shift."

"Oh," Frank said. "How's that going? Last time we talked you said you really loved it."

"I still do," Ginny said as everyone finished up eating.

"You won't believe what happened at the hospital the other day," Ginny said later as they

33

walked out of the Cave. Frank was on one side, Liz on the other. As they crossed the quad, Ginny talked excitedly about her experiences in the pediatric wing. Experiences she had longed to share with Ray.

"I love dancing with you!" Tim Downing shouted to Kara over the sound of the jukebox in the Underground. The guys from Blue Suspense were on a break, and students were crowding the small dance floor.

"Ditto!" Kara shouted, her long sun-streaked brown hair swinging across her face as she moved to the heavy beat of the music. She loved doing just about anything with Tim. Being with the cute Alpha Delt freshman was always fun and made Kara very happy.

The music ended, and someone switched off the jukebox. "The band's warming up again," Tim said, leading Kara back to the table they were sharing with Montana and Nikki.

"Blue Suspense is really a good group," Montana said as Tim made his way to the bar to get another round of sodas.

Kara nodded. "Wish they were from around here. Especially with the Beat Poets getting ready to record. They'll be too busy for campus gigs."

"Where are they now?" Nikki asked.

Kara laughed. "Off in Chicago for a recording session or something like that."

"Ah—so that explains *that!*" Montana interjected, and elbowed Kara in the ribs.

"Explains what?" Kara asked, then followed Montana's gaze to a table across the room. "Oh, Ginny's here."

"But look who she's with—I mean, what's up? Ray's out of town, and she's with another guy."

Kara rolled her eyes. "Montana, I wouldn't call having a conversation with Frank Chung being 'with him.' "

"But what's with her and Ray?" Nikki asked. "I haven't seen them together lately."

Kara sighed. "They haven't been—actually." She dropped her voice. "I don't think everyone knows about it yet, but they've split up."

"Oh?" Montana leaned forward toward Kara. "Why?"

Kara shrugged. "I don't know the details, only that it's a temporary split."

"Doesn't look temporary to me," Montana said, with a meaningful nod toward Ginny and Frank.

"I can't imagine Ginny with Frank instead of Ray," Nikki blurted out. "Frank's a nice guy, but Ray, well, he's so cool and such a great singer."

"I'm sure she's not dating Frank," Kara stated.

Montana just shrugged and gave a little smile. "Interesting, though."

Kara studied Montana a minute. Why did she look happy about Ginny and Ray's breakup? Before she could give it another thought, Tim came back.

"Tomorrow's the big day," he said, depositing the sodas on the table. "Aren't you guys nervous about your radio gig?" he asked.

"Nervous?" Montana laughed. "Psyched, yes. Nervous, no. Right, guys?"

Kara gulped. "Wrong. I'm nervous. By the way, did you ever pick up that envelope at the Pi Phi desk, Nikki? The one Patrice left with this week's topic?"

"You don't know what you're talking about on the air yet?" Tim started to laugh.

"No sweat," Montana said, pulling an envelope out of her bag. "I picked it up already."

"But you haven't opened it." Tim sounded amazed.

"It's better not to think about the topic too much," Montana replied, tearing open the envelope. "I want to sound spontaneous." She stared at the memo in her hand. "Ughhhh!" she exclaimed, and shoved the paper across the table.

" 'Should there be more women in student government?' " Kara read aloud. "Gimme a break."

Nikki flopped her head forward in her arms. "BORING!" she said loudly into the tabletop.

Tim chuckled. "Patrice is sure a pill. Talk about dry!" He laughed outright.

"This is not funny, Tim," Kara protested, feeling pretty awful. "Of all subjects—why, last week she had a much better topic."

"Right—frat parties and dress codes. But this . . ." Nikki wailed.

"We can do better," Montana said, yanking the slip of paper from Kara's hand and crushing it into a little ball.

"You mean we should make up our own?" Nikki sounded astounded.

"I'm game." Kara thought a moment. "How about the pros and cons of a coed football squad?"

"Spare me!" Tim moaned.

"Admit it—that would be controversial," Montana said. "Or remember that article in the *Wilder Times* about having TV monitors in classrooms instead of teachers? The professors would tape lectures, and then the university could hire fewer teachers."

"We could have fun with it," Kara suggested. "A really crazy discussion about professors being hired only after a screen test."

"Seriously, Kara, you've got to come up with something to talk about," Tim said.

"Not to worry!" Kara exclaimed. "We will. We've got until tomorrow afternoon."

"Kara's right. There's lots of time between now and then for inspiration to strike," Nikki said.

"Inspiration?" Tim mouthed the word at Kara.

"Of course, Tim, you've got to have a little faith in us. We're a mighty powerful threesome when we put our minds to it," Kara said.

"For your sake, I hope so," Tim whispered in her ear, then gently nuzzled her neck.

Kara didn't answer. She lifted her face toward Tim's, and the smell of his aftershave drove all thoughts of the next day's radio talk show right out of her head.

* * *

"Dinner will be ready in five minutes," Hannah said from the Drews' dining room that evening. Will, George, and Bess had joined Jake, Nancy, Avery, and Carson Drew in the living room for hors d'oeuvres.

"Let me help!" Nancy exclaimed from the sofa, where she was sitting between her father and Jake. Before she could get up, her father was on his feet.

"No, you don't," he said, grinning down at his daughter. "I want you to stay put and enjoy being with your friends. Avery and I have everything under control." He reached out and pulled Avery up from the floor, where she had been sitting next to Will and George.

"You bet," Avery agreed, brushing off her slim-fitting pants and adjusting her gray cashmere sweater over her slender hips. The sweater matched her huge smoky eyes, and Nancy could understand exactly why her father had fallen in love with Avery at first sight. She was beautiful, with shoulder-length glossy brown hair and a calm air that Nancy found very appealing.

"But I like helping Hannah," Nancy protested

"Nancy—this is your night off. Besides, there's a little surprise."

Nancy forced a smile. "Okay."

"They're like two kids together," Jake remarked as Carson Drew and Avery went hand-in-hand through the dining room.

"Uh-huh," Nancy said distractedly. She followed Avery and her father with her eyes.

"Nancy," George said, "I never thought I'd see your dad in love like this. He looks so happy."

Nancy nodded. "Yes," she said vaguely, then, hearing herself, she frowned. *"Yes!"* she repeated more emphatically. "He's been alone too long. And Avery's great—she really is."

George laughed. "Remember when you first met her, the day your dad brought her to Wilder? You were so scared you wouldn't like her."

"But I did—I do," Nancy said. And it was true. Still, Nancy hadn't expected Avery here tonight. Part of her had looked forward to spending the evening just with her friends and her dad, the way they used to. Silly of me, she chided herself, but she couldn't quite shake her annoyance.

A moment later her father reappeared, carrying a tray of hot hors d'oeuvres.

"Wow," Will said. "Those smell great."

"I'll bet they taste even better," Jake said, popping one in his mouth.

Nancy eyed them hungrily. "Hannah has outdone herself this time."

"Hannah didn't make these," Carson Drew said, pride sounding in his voice. "Avery did."

Avery's face glowed.

"Believe me, they're really special," he added, handing a miniature quiche to Nancy.

"Nice," she said halfheartedly.

George, Will, and Jake were all complimenting Avery. Jake was getting along well with her dad's girlfriend. Good, Nancy thought, again without much enthusiasm.

What's wrong with me? she wondered. Nancy realized that Bess wasn't in the room. Grabbing a quiche from the tray, she set out to locate Bess.

Nancy found her friend curled up on the couch in the den, staring transfixed at the TV screen.

"Want a quiche?" Nancy asked.

"Uh—no."

Nancy settled down next to Bess and looked at her out of the corner of her eye. She frowned. Bess's face was a blank. Even though she was staring at the TV, she didn't seem to be really focused on it. "So, what's on the tube?"

"Not much, a news show doing a story on the recording industry."

"Anything interesting?" Nancy asked.

Bess shrugged. "I don't know. I haven't actually been following it," Bess said. Nancy noticed again the flatness in Bess's voice.

Nancy was thinking about having a heart-to-heart talk with Bess when the TV reporter's voice caught her attention.

"Of course, the biggest problem for the companies and recording artists is posed by counterfeiters. Cybersounds is just one of a number of bands who've been victims of counterfeit CDs and tapes lately . . ."

"Counterfeit?" Nancy murmured out loud. She looked toward Bess.

Bess had her head back against the couch, her eyes closed. Nancy listened as the reporter explained how Cybersounds' latest recording wasn't due for release until the following week, but counterfeit tapes had already surfaced all over the country, seriously cutting into the band's sales.

"Chow's on!" Avery called from the living room.

"Just a minute," Nancy said, wanting to hear more. But the station cut to a commercial.

"Weird!" Nancy said, half to herself, as Bess got up and they headed out of the den.

"What?" Bess said. "I sort of dozed off."

"Oh, nothing, really," Nancy said, thinking how tired Bess looked. But as they joined the others in the dining room, Nancy couldn't help but wonder about those Cybersounds tapes Jake had found in the duffel bag.

Could they be counterfeits? And how did the owner get hold of them?

CHAPTER 4

Jonathan," Stephanie Keats cooed as she and Jonathan Bauer drove toward the campus. "It's too early to call it a night."

They'd just left the Weston movie theater, but Stephanie couldn't recall the name of the film. For Stephanie it had been a stars-in-your-eyes romance starring her and Jonathan as they shared kiss after steamy kiss.

Now she reached across the front seat and ran one well-manicured nail gently down the side of his cheek. She could feel his pulse quicken.

"So, where to?" Jonathan asked. He took one hand off the wheel and wrapped his arm around her.

She leaned her head into his palm and thanked her lucky stars she had taken that part-time job at Berrigan's. If she hadn't, she'd never have met

Jonathan, who worked as a floor manager there. "The lake should look beautiful in the moonlight."

Jonathan laughed and glanced away from the road a moment. His dark eyes shone. "Sounds good."

Jonathan pulled into the lakeside parking lot and flicked out the headlights. Stephanie unhooked her seat belt and slid closer to Jonathan. She watched his devilishly handsome face in the moonlight.

He leaned down and grazed her lips with a kiss, then reached across the seat and opened her door. "Let's take a walk."

"A walk?" she repeated, disappointed.

With a sigh, she climbed out of the car. "Do we *have* to—walk?" she said in a sultry voice, taking his hand and holding him back a little.

Jonathan dropped her hand. "I want to talk."

"About what?" Stephanie's guard went up.

"Us. We barely know each other." Jonathan flashed a half-smile that made her knees go weak. Then he started for the lake.

"How can you say that?" she shot back, not following him. "I'd say we've been getting pretty close lately."

Jonathan turned around. "Hey, Steph, don't get so defensive. You know how much I like you."

Did she? Stephanie suddenly had doubts.

He retraced his steps until he stood in front of

her. He ran his hand up the side of her face and tangled his fingers in her hair.

Stephanie caught her breath and touched his lips with her finger. "Why waste time talking?"

"Not now," he said. He took her hand away from his face but continued to hold it tight. He started back toward the lake, and Stephanie stayed right beside him.

"Well, then," she said, wondering why she felt afraid. "What do you want to talk about?"

Jonathan shrugged. "Stuff. Ordinary stuff. We've been friends for a while now."

"Friends?" Stephanie's eyebrow shot up.

"Not *just* friends."

She wanted to counter with something smart and fast and witty. Instead she heard herself admit, "I'm not used to 'talking' with guys. I always wonder if they'd stick around once they knew the real me."

"I will," Jonathan said, sending her heart soaring.

A second later Jonathan chuckled. "Tell you what. I'll tell you one of my dumb childhood secrets. You tell me one of yours."

"Why?" Stephanie scoffed.

"So I can get to know the 'real' you better." Jonathan slipped his hands down her arms and tugged her toward him. "Come on."

Stephanie couldn't help but return his smile. "Okay. You first, though."

Jonathan stopped walking. "Hmmmm—well, when I was about ten, I ran away from home."

"You did? Why?"

Jonathan let out a full-throated laugh. "Because my big brother wouldn't let me tag along to his high school prom."

"Do you blame him?" Stephanie laughed, trying to picture the muscled man beside her as a kid.

Jonathan looked at Stephanie. "Your turn."

"Do I *have* to?"

"Yup."

Stephanie swallowed hard and tried to think. She wanted to share something, but something safe, not something she'd regret.

"When I was ten . . ." she started, and then knew she couldn't go on. She didn't know what was safe to share. So she made something up.

"I wanted to be a track and field star." Actually, as far back as she could remember, Stephanie had hated gym or sports or anything that got her hair messed up. With that, she slipped out of Jonathan's reach and began running.

"No fair," he yelled, and ran after her. She slowed and dropped to the grass. Jonathan threw himself down next to her. The grass was damp and cold, but Stephanie didn't care.

"You copped out!" he accused.

"Yeah—I guess I did," she said, gasping to catch her breath. Jonathan didn't give her a chance.

He lowered his face over hers and practically smothered her with a long, deep kiss. They broke for air, and he whispered, "Stephanie, you owe me one."

"One what?" she whispered back, pretending not to understand.

"One childhood secret."

"There's plenty of time for that," she said, hoping with her whole heart it would be true. She longed to know him long enough to share all her childhood secrets, every single one. But right now all she wanted to share was one more kiss.

As their lips met Stephanie felt every bit of herself go into meltdown.

Jake leaned back from kissing Nancy and stared into her eyes. "Why do I have the feeling you're not all here?" he murmured huskily.

"I'm all here," Nancy said, tightening her arms around his neck and sliding closer on the couch.

Hannah, Carson Drew, and Avery had turned in for the evening. Jake and Nancy had retreated to the den, where Nancy dimmed the lights and lit candles on the top of the desk. Her hair gleamed in the candlelight, and her cheeks were pink from the warmth of the room. Jake thought she looked achingly beautiful. But her eyes were vaguely unfocused and distant-looking.

Jake felt Nancy press her head against his chest and run her hand up his arm. She absently fingered the suede patch on the elbow of the sweater he had borrowed from her father and laughed softly.

"My father's clothes are definitely *not* your style," Nancy said.

Jake pretended to be hurt. "And what would my style be?" he asked.

"I'm not sure, but whatever it is, it's very sexy." Nancy leaned over and kissed his cheek.

"Tomorrow I'd better pick up a pair of jeans and some other stuff," Jake said.

"We'll go to the mall first thing."

"Right," Jake replied. "Let's check out the new one. That's where Nick's uncle has his record store."

"It'll be fun to see Nick," Nancy said. Suddenly she sat up. "Oh, I wanted to tell you about something. Bess had the TV on in here before dinner—"

Jake interrupted. "I noticed she'd left."

Nancy's face clouded over. "Bess is a mess," she said. "She's walking around like the living dead. And she won't talk about Paul or anything. Not with me. Not with George."

Jake didn't know what to say to that. Nancy was quiet for a moment before continuing.

"Anyway, Bess was watching this news show on the recording industry, and the reporter started talking about counterfeit CDs and tapes. Cybersounds was one of the bands mentioned as being ripped off. The report said that their new album isn't being released until next week, but it's already being counterfeited and is selling all over the country on the black market."

Jake stared at Nancy. "You're kidding!"

Nancy shook her head.

"Those tapes we found in the bag, Nan, they've got to be ripoffs. Don't you think?"

"Seems like it."

Jake leaned back and propped his arms behind his head. "Maybe we've stumbled into a really hot story with this stuff."

Nancy didn't respond; she was staring at the candles again. He felt she hadn't heard a word he'd just said.

"Nancy?" He put his hand under her chin and turned her face to his. "You look like something's bothering you. Is it the tapes?"

"The tapes?" she repeated, then said absently, "No, it's nothing."

Jake grabbed her hand and drew her closer. He smiled at her. Slowly she smiled back, then leaned into Jake for a long, sweet kiss. When they surfaced for air a few minutes later, Nancy propped her back against Jake's chest and sighed.

"You're sure you're okay?" he asked.

"Hmmmm." She sounded content, and Jake's smile widened.

"I really like being in your home, meeting your dad and Hannah." He straightened up and met Nancy's eyes. "She's great."

"She's been like a mother to me," Nancy said, sounding almost wistful.

"And now there's Avery."

"Avery? My *mother*?" Nancy sounded annoyed.

Jake blinked. He looked hard at Nancy, then

began to laugh. "I guess not. She's not old enough."

Nancy looked contrite. She gave an embarrassed laugh. "Really! And I don't think my father would expect me to think of her as a mother, either. But," she added in the next breath, "I really like her."

"Me, too," Jake agreed, but he noticed that Nancy still seemed preoccupied.

They sat in silence a moment.

"I'm glad for my father," she suddenly blurted out.

"How could you not be?"

Nancy looked up at Jake. Her smile still wasn't up to full wattage. He reached out and touched her lips. "He's almost as lucky as I was when I met you." Before she could answer, he sealed her lips with a kiss.

Saturday morning Ray walked into the Chicago recording studio, ready to take on the world.

He hung his jacket on the coatrack in the reception area and grinned when he noticed that Spider's coat was already hanging there.

Spider had driven his van from Weston with the band's manager, Roger Hall, who also happened to be Spider's brother-in-law. Ray and the rest of the guys had come up in Bruce's car.

"This place is awesome," Denny Curtis, the band's bass player, said as he swung through the door. He hung his denim jacket, emblazoned with rock band logos, next to Ray's.

Sam Dixon's motorcycle boots clunked across the shiny wood floor as he checked out his drum set. "Spider got here earlier, huh?"

"Where are they, anyway?" Bruce Kincaid said.

"Somewhere. Let's check things out," Ray said.

A receptionist unlocked the recording studio door and turned on the power and lights. Ray carefully leaned his guitar against one of the studio walls.

"Hey!" Spider called across the room.

Ray glanced up. Spider looked excited, and there was a bounce in his step as he approached.

"All right!" He slapped Ray five.

Ray returned his grin and nodded amiably at Roger Hall, who was standing behind Spider.

"Hello," Roger said. He walked over to the sound booth, where an engineer was manning the equipment.

"The time clock's running, guys. And time here really does mean money," Ray heard Roger say.

"Hey, Joel," Spider called out.

Ray turned and saw an older man dressed casually in jeans and a denim shirt walk in.

"Ray," Spider said, "this is Joel Hoffman."

"You flew in today?" Ray asked pleasantly, and shook the executive's hand.

"Yes," Joel said. "Good to meet you at last. I really liked what I heard on the demo tapes. The Beat Poets certainly has a great sound."

Ray flushed with pleasure. "Thanks." Ray introduced Joel to the other members of the group.

After a few minutes of instrument tuning and sound checks, the band broke into a hard-driving tune. It was an electric rhythm-and-blues number that Ray had written. Four measures into the music, Ray leaned into the mike and belted the hard-edged lyrics in his raspy voice.

Ray and Spider switched to acoustic guitars and the more mellow sound that made them Wilder's favorite band.

Ray sang one of the heartfelt songs he had written with Ginny. For a moment he actually imagined her in the room with him. He could feel all the love they once shared.

Ray opened his eyes. There was, of course, no Ginny. The pain of their separation spurred him into his best singing.

At the end of the song, he knew that the band had been inspired by his performance. He turned, and the others gave him a high sign. The whole band knew what they had just pulled off. Ray felt fantastic.

He looked through the glass partition that separated the recording studio from the engineer's station. Joel and Roger were sitting with their heads together, looking in his direction. Both men were frowning.

A prickly sensation ran up the back of Ray's neck. He had a gut feeling that something weird was going on. But, he asked himself as the band began to retune the instruments, what?

*   *   *

The next morning Nancy woke up to the smell of pancakes and sausage wafting up from the kitchen.

She was out of bed in a shot, and as she headed for the shower, she realized she felt better. Whatever had been bothering her about Avery the night before was over. Why shouldn't Avery be there? Nancy was determined to have a fresh and open attitude toward Avery the next time she saw her.

Fifteen minutes later Nancy bounded down the stairs. She poked her head in the dining room and stared. "Avery?" she said, startled to find her at the breakfast table.

Avery looked up from her pancakes. "Hi, Nancy."

"Morning, hon," her father said.

Jake tilted his chair back. "Hey," he said.

"Hello," she managed. She reminded herself that she had known Avery would be there. Instead of driving back to her condo, she had spent the night, and her father had told Nancy that Avery would stay the weekend.

Nancy poured herself a cup of coffee from the pot on the buffet. Jake made room for her next to him at the table.

"Here's round two!" Hannah announced, walking into the room. "Good morning, Nan." Hannah smiled at her but stopped first at Avery's plate and heaped it high with pancakes.

"Hannah, you're stuffing me." But as Nancy watched, Avery dug in.

"You must work out." Nancy tried to smile.

Avery nodded. "Believe me, it's a good thing I do. I really love to eat, especially when Hannah's cooking."

"I love cooking for you." Hannah looked at Nancy. "It hasn't been the same around here with Nancy gone—until you came along."

Hannah stopped at Nancy's plate. "Hungry?"

"Not really," Nancy said curtly. She motioned the pancakes away.

"Not hungry for my pancakes?"

Jake laughed. "I'll take what she doesn't."

Nancy sipped some coffee. For a few seconds, light chatter and laughter went on at the table. Nancy barely took in a word.

"Nancy." Her father touched her arm. "So, what do you think?"

Nancy colored. "Uh, I sort of tuned out of the conversation."

"About my study . . ." Carson Drew looked at Nancy. "I said that since Avery did such a great job redecorating her condo, I asked her to help me start redecorating my study."

"Redecorating?" Nancy said, her chest tightening. "Why?"

"Everything's a little shabby," he said. "It's time for a change."

"We've even picked out a great color scheme," Avery said with a big smile. "Although it took some talking to get Carson to agree to the new colors."

Nancy looked at Avery, who had one hand

resting lightly on her father's arm. Avery continued, "I had to convince him. Carson's color sense seems to be limited to shades of gray and brown."

"But not now. I'm a changed man," he said, looking at her adoringly.

"Right. I found the most wonderful blue rug—not a navy blue, but a kind of deep—"

"Blue?" Nancy repeated. "I think that's completely wrong. Your study will look awful. But who needs my opinion, anyway?"

Her father's fork stopped halfway to his mouth. Avery's eyes widened. Nancy balled up her napkin and stood up. "I'm going to see what Hannah's up to in the kitchen."

She pushed through the swinging door and was enveloped in the familiar, warm, sweet smells of the kitchen. "Hannah," she said, walking over to the sink and putting one arm around the salt-and-pepper-haired housekeeper. "I've missed you."

"Me, too," Hannah said, pulling Nancy in for a long, warm hug.

Now, this felt like home, Nancy thought.

She began helping Hannah load the dishwasher. "I've even missed doing this."

Hannah laughed. "Never thought I'd hear *you* say that."

Nancy thought a moment. "Yeah—I've never been much for cleaning or cooking, even though you've tried your best to teach me."

"You're good enough at it," Hannah said.

"But some people, like Avery, just love cooking."

Nancy's smile dimmed.

"You know, she's wonderful for your father. He's really fallen in love."

"Right." Nancy threw some forks in the silverware basket. The big rattling noise was particularly satisfying.

"I've never seen him so happy."

"I'm sure." Nancy banged a cabinet door shut.

"Nancy?" Hannah stared at her from the sink.

Nancy drew in her breath sharply. "Look, it's getting late," she said. "I promised Jake we'd get over to the mall as soon as it opened."

"Hi," Jake said, coming into the kitchen.

"Jake, let's split. Now," Nancy said tightly.

"What's the rush?" he asked, following her out the side kitchen door that led into the hall.

Nancy grabbed her purse from the coatrack. "It's a beautiful day. I can't stand being inside."

"Nancy, what's wrong?" he asked.

Nancy took a deep breath. "I'm uncomfortable having Avery here." That wasn't quite right, but Nancy couldn't put her feelings into words yet. She lifted her eyes to Jake, hoping he would help her figure it all out.

"Avery?" He looked startled. "You were a little hard on her at the table."

Nancy couldn't miss the slightly critical tone in his voice. "Don't you get it, Jake? I'm not used to having some girlfriend of my father here at home, acting like she's part of the family."

"But your father is happy," he said. "And you really liked Avery back at Wilder."

Nancy needed Jake to understand her. "I do like her. But that was *there*. Here, it's weird. I mean, the way Hannah dotes on her."

"Avery's terrific. Maybe you're upset about something else. About Bess."

Nancy stared at Jake in disbelief. "Of course I'm upset about Bess. But I'm not talking about Bess. I'm talking about Avery."

"Avery," Jake said, "seems to be making everyone happy but you."

Right! Nancy felt her patience growing thin. She tried to think of another way to make Jake understand as she headed for the driver's side of her car. Jake opened the passenger door.

"I thought I locked that last night," Nancy said distractedly.

"When everyone rushed out to say hello, you probably forgot."

"Probably," Nancy said. "Jake, about Avery. Can't you see why I'm feeling this way?"

Jake reached over to turn on the tape deck, but Nancy stopped him. She wanted to talk this out while they drove to the mall. Nancy felt extremely frustrated. The one person she wanted to understand her didn't know what she meant.

CHAPTER 5

Saturday morning George bounded off the hiking path at the Keelor Falls Nature Preserve and scaled the rocky slope. "Come on, Will," she called back over her shoulder. "I want to show you something."

"Ah—another landmark on my George Fayne hometown tour," Will replied, his cheeks pink from the wind and exercise.

George grinned down into Will's chiseled features, then continued up the hill. At the peak she jumped up onto a low, flat outcropping of rock and stopped to catch her breath. George leaned against a tree and waited for Will. She was dying to see his reaction. The rock overlooked the spot where the Keelor River churned in whitewater froth, then finally became Keelor Falls as it spilled over the twenty-five-foot drop.

"It's a little slippery," George warned.

"Awesome!" Will shouted over the waterfall.

"Do you love it or what?" George asked.

"Definitely!" Will slung both his arms around George's neck and pressed his forehead against hers. He leaned against the tree trunk, with George in front of him. Together they watched the falls in silence.

"I could stay here forever," Will said, nestling his cheek on top of George's head.

George couldn't answer. Sometimes Will just took her breath away. She had never loved anyone this much.

"So, where are all the other people?" he asked a little huskily.

George turned around in his arms. "Why?" she said, her heart pounding.

"We seem to be alone and off the beaten path and . . ."

The sound of voices and laughter carried clearly over the roar of the water. "Would you believe it, someone's coming," George said grumpily. "There's another approach to the falls from the fairgrounds."

A second later a man and a woman emerged from the woods a little south of Will and George. "George!" The girl waved as they scrambled onto the rock.

"Kate? Jeff?" George untangled herself from Will's arms.

"Hi, you two."

"Jeff," Kate said. "This is Will."

Jeff shook Will's hand and said, "This place is outta sight! How come we didn't meet up on the path?"

"We took the hard way up here," Will joked. Kate chuckled.

"So, how do you know about this place?" Will asked. "Are you from River Heights, too?"

Jeff shook his head. "No. We're here for the Keelor Falls Festival. I'm selling tapes and earrings at it. A friend mentioned this place."

"We wanted to spend the day relaxing before the festival tomorrow," Kate said.

"It's nice to be free on a Saturday for a change," Jeff added. "If I'm not studying, I'm usually working some street fair or festival."

Jeff's comments about the festival jogged George's memory.

"Right—the festival!" She turned to Jeff. "You won't believe this, but a friend of ours, Jake Collins, grabbed the wrong duffel bag yesterday from the lobby of Thayer Hall. It was full of brand-new, unopened audio tapes and a flier for the Keelor Falls Festival, too," George said. "Did you misplace a bag?"

"Not me," Jeff answered.

"Our stuff's packed in Jeff's van." Kate motioned toward the parking lot below.

"Too bad. I hope the owner of the bag doesn't need it this weekend," George said, then got another idea. "But maybe," she asked Jeff, "you know someone else from the street fair crowd who's planning on being here and selling tapes. Someone from school?"

"No, I don't," Jeff said quickly, and checked his watch. "Hey, we'd better get moving."

Kate frowned. "So fast? It's beautiful here, and I was going to ask George and Will to have lunch with us."

"Maybe some other time," Jeff said. "I've got a few things to do for the festival."

Kate gave a disappointed shrug as she waved goodbye to George and Will.

"That was odd!" George remarked, watching the couple walk off through the woods.

"Running into them like that?" Will asked.

"Having to leave so suddenly," George said. "Why'd he get so nervous?"

"I didn't really notice," Will replied. "Maybe he's a nervous kind of guy."

"Maybe," George conceded without much conviction. George didn't know Jeff well, but the last word she'd use to describe him was *nervous*.

When Jake and Nancy arrived at the West Side Mall, the parking lot was nearly full, and Ed's Music World was mobbed. The record store's windows were festooned with red, white, and blue plastic banners announcing a grand opening sale.

The upbeat, almost manic atmosphere lifted Nancy's spirits. As she and Jake jostled to get into the store, her frustration over Avery faded away.

"Glad we headed here first," Jake said.

Nancy agreed, looking around. Two or three guys were at the cash registers, and a young woman was sorting CDs into bins. "I don't see Nick," she said. "You sure this is the right store?"

Jake nodded. "Even when we do find him, he won't have time to hang out with us."

Just then Nancy spotted Jake's roommate coming out of a back room. "Nick!" she yelled.

Nick looked up and waved. "Isn't this something?" he said. "Ed, that's my uncle, he's up there by the cash register. It's crazy in here, huh?"

Nancy craned her neck and spotted the man who must have been Nick's uncle immediately. He was middle-aged and a little shorter than Nick, but their faces were very similar.

"You're not kidding," Jake said.

Before he could say more, a boy walked up. "Excuse me," he said to Nick. "Do you work here?"

"Yes. Can I help you?"

"I'm looking for the Cybersounds' new album," the teenager said.

Nick checked a printout hanging on the wall. "It's not out until next week. Come back then. Remember, we always run a good discount."

"No, dude, you must be wrong," the boy insisted. "My buddy Sean picked the tape up here just yesterday."

Nick seemed puzzled and was starting to say

something when his uncle walked up. "What's the problem?"

"Uncle Ed, this guy says that the Cybersounds' new album is out, and someone bought a tape of it here. When?"

"Yesterday," the teenager insisted.

"But it's not due for release until next week," Nick continued.

As Nancy watched, Ed frowned. "Cybersounds? No. Can't be," Nick's uncle said with a nervous smile. "Not if it's not due out for a week." Then he accompanied the boy toward the front of the store. "Anything else you want I've probably got." Over the general din, Nancy couldn't hear more.

But, she reflected as Nick and Jake continued talking, Nick's uncle Ed looked uncomfortable at the mention of the Cybersounds tape.

Before she could give it a second thought, she caught sight of a very familiar tall, dark-haired figure heading for a display of jazz CDs.

"Ned!" she gasped, and a second later was in his arms sharing a strong hug. They stepped back and smiled at each other.

"Nancy, what are you doing here?" Ned's smooth, familiar voice was music to her ears.

"We've got a long weekend—no classes until Tuesday. George is here, too, with Will. How about you?" Nancy couldn't believe it would feel so good, so comfortable, seeing Ned again.

"No, I just don't have Monday classes this

term," Ned said. "I drove down from school to visit my parents. I didn't expect to see you."

"Nancy?" Jake had walked up behind her and put his hand on her shoulder. Ned's eyebrows lifted slightly.

"Oh, Jake," Nancy said, suddenly feeling a little flustered. "This is my old friend, Ned Nickerson. Ned, this is Jake Collins."

"I've heard about you. You're at Emerson," Jake replied easily, not missing a beat. He put his hand out to Ned.

Nancy watched Ned take Jake in. "Yes," he answered.

Nancy relaxed. Ned seemed easy, casual.

"Jake's a junior. We work together on the paper," she said. She looked from Jake to Ned. Both guys were handsome. Jake had a sexy, boyish look about him. Ned was a little taller and more muscular, with a square-jawed face. He looked, Nancy thought with a tug at her heart, very handsome.

"Hey, I've got to check with Nick about something, Nancy. Great meeting you, Ned," Jake said. He walked back to the far end of the store, where Nick was labeling some tapes.

"Nice guy," Ned said.

"Yes, he is," Nancy hesitated, then peered into Ned's dark eyes. "I'm glad you think so."

"What's going on with Bess?" Ned asked.

"She's here, recuperating at home."

"Of course," Ned said, his face showing concern. "How is she?"

"She's fine, at least physically. Her arm's mending, though she's still a little sore. But"—Nancy paused to put her thoughts together—"she's not doing well emotionally. George and I thought she'd at least want to talk to us—cry with us, something. But all she's doing is watching TV like some kind of zombie."

"I'll call her right away," Ned said worriedly. He studied Nancy a moment. "You haven't mentioned the other news."

"What news?" Nancy asked, puzzled.

"About your dad and a certain woman lawyer. My parents are really excited about it."

"Oh, *that,*" Nancy said, her spirits sinking.

"You don't like her?" Ned sounded surprised.

"Oh, Ned, I do. I did. I don't know," Nancy admitted miserably.

"This doesn't sound like you," Ned said, joking, but his concern showed in his eyes.

"I met Avery a while ago when Dad brought her to Wilder, and I loved her. But this weekend, seeing her in my house, taking over, beginning to redecorate. Would you believe it, she's redoing my dad's study? I don't know. . . ."

"She's taking over your territory," Ned said.

Nancy's heart lifted. "You understand!"

"You've had your dad, Hannah, and the whole house to yourself for more than fifteen years, Nancy. It's tough to make way for a new person in your family."

"That's it," Nancy said.

"But that's normal. I'm sure you'll get over it.

It'll just take a little time to adjust. I wouldn't worry about it. You don't have to love the situation right away. You'll get used to Avery. My parents say she's really wonderful."

"True," Nancy conceded. She felt so happy to see Ned again. "Thanks for understanding."

"But what about Bess, anything special you think I should say to her?" he asked as they headed toward the register, where Jake was buying some tapes.

"I asked her to come to dinner and a club later with Jake, George, Will, and me, but she said no. Maybe you could get her to change her mind." Without a second thought, Nancy added, "And that means, of course, you'd come, too."

"I'd like that," Ned said.

"George would really love to see you again."

"Okay," Ned said, heading for the door. "I'll work my magic and bring Bess."

Nancy didn't miss Ned's quick glance in Jake's direction. "Jake won't mind, Ned," Nancy said. Jake was too confident of her feelings for him to be jealous of an old boyfriend.

"Disasterville, that's what this is!" Kara wailed a few minutes before noon Saturday. She, Montana, and Nikki were alone in Wilder's KWDR radio station. Ten minutes more, and the Saturday call-in show would begin, or, Kara thought wryly, it was *supposed* to begin.

That is, if anyone could figure out how to turn on the mikes and use the control panel.

"Montana?" Nikki cried. "I thought you knew what you were doing here!"

"I do," Montana said tightly. She shook her mane of blond curls back from her face and frowned down at the three headsets with tangled wires draped over her arm.

Montana had assigned each girl a job when they'd stumbled into the studio half an hour earlier, groggy from spending an all-nighter in Nikki's Pi Phi room trying to figure out what to talk about on the air. They hadn't come up with a topic yet.

Kara's job was to find the list of commercials and the log book to sign in and out. So far, Kara had checked every drawer, countertop, and pegboard in sight and had come up empty.

Nikki was looking bewildered in front of the control panel, trying to get the mikes on.

"We could," Nikki suggested, looking as frazzled as she sounded, "use that topic about women in student government."

"No way!" Montana declared, finally unsnarling the headsets.

"Montana's right," Kara seconded. She had wanted to be a talk-show host too long to make her debut with such a boring subject. She continued to search for the logbooks.

Nikki sank back in a swivel desk chair and began fiddling nervously with switches on the control panel. Montana made a calming gesture with both her hands. "Cool it, guys! This is no time for panic attacks."

"Right," Nikki said. "My mom always says to take ten deep breaths to relieve stress."

"Forget about deep breaths," Montana cried. "There's no time. Seven minutes and we're on!"

"Where are those time logs?" Kara dove under a table and began searching the trash. As she hunted, Kara tried to remember the topics they'd come up with the night before. She drew a complete blank. When she looked up, Nikki was still at the control panel, bewildered. "Nikki!" Kara cried. "Haven't you figured that out yet?"

"I'm making a systematic check here, but none of this is working like Montana said it would," Nikki said, pulling a switch. Ear-splitting feedback vibrated across the studio. All three girls shrieked at once and clamped their hands over their ears. Kara quickly reached over and flipped the switch off.

"Wait, I remember now," Montana said, leaning over the control panel. "This switch first, then that. And those knobs control the volume."

"Montana," Nikki said in a voice filled with despair, "I thought you knew how to run all this."

"I do—sort of—but this setup is far more complicated than the studio back at Northside High."

Montana turned a couple of knobs and buttons. There was no feedback, but the red on-air light flicked on a moment. Montana flicked off the switch, and the on-air sign went out.

Kara began to relax. Nikki was testing the mike, and everything seemed okay.

"I think we've got it under control," Montana said. "Now, if I could only remember what Patrice said about the FCC rules." She looked helplessly toward Kara and Nikki.

Nikki wrinkled her delicate nose. "I think there was something about giving the call letters, but I don't remember when."

"Or how often?" Montana said with a big sigh. "Patrice told us, but I forgot. Kara?"

Kara shifted uneasily in her chair. "I tuned out on the tech stuff. I thought you had it all under control. I was going over the jokes I'd make."

"Jokes about what?" Nikki asked. "We don't even know what we're going to talk about yet."

"I know, and"—Kara pointed to the clock hanging near the studio door—"it's just two minutes until airtime."

"What a great day!" Nancy exclaimed as she and Jake sauntered out of the main entrance of the mall. They were laden with shopping bags: CDs and tapes from Ed's store, clothes and shaving supplies for Jake, and a new dress for Nancy. She was sure Jake would like the color; it matched her eyes perfectly.

"Shopping sure cheered you up," Jake remarked, shifting all his bags to one hand and reaching for Nancy's hand with the other.

Nancy returned the pressure of his hand. Yes, she was feeling happier than she had earlier. As they crossed the parking lot toward her Mustang, Nancy still wished Jake would understand about

Avery, but maybe she was expecting too much. She and Jake had known each other only two months or so. How could he know her every thought and mood?

Nancy glanced at Jake sideways, and her mouth softened into a smile. They still had so much to learn about each other.

Nancy put the car key in the lock. "Hey, what's this?" The paint around the lock was scratched.

Jake came around to the driver's side and asked, "When did that happen?"

"I don't know." Nancy tried the key. The lock was still locked. She opened the door and checked inside. "Jake, did you take the tapes into the house last night?"

"No. Everyone came out to say hello, then I grabbed the bags and brought them inside. Some of the tapes were beside the seat."

"I was afraid of that. They're gone."

"What?"

"Look for yourself." Nancy knelt on the driver's seat and pressed the eject button on the tape deck. Nothing came out. "Look, even the Cybersounds tape in the deck is gone."

Jake frowned. "Were they here this morning?"

Nancy tried to remember. "I didn't notice one way or the other. We didn't play music on the way to the mall," she reminded him.

"Right," Jake said, "we were talking the whole way here." Jake looked at the chipped paint around the car lock. "But how could the car be broken into if the door was still locked?"

Nancy nodded. "Just what I was wondering. But it was definitely locked. You just saw me open it. But someone did break into the car and steal those tapes." She sighed, knowing it was hopeless to think the thief would still be hanging around. They'd been at the mall for hours. Someone could have broken in right after they arrived.

Still, Nancy glanced around the parking lot. She saw a familiar figure hurrying toward a door to the mall.

"Look," she said. "Isn't that Nick's uncle?" Nancy noticed a small brown box tucked under Ed Dimartini's arm. He was holding what appeared to be a couple of cassette tapes. Before he went through the door, he slowed and suddenly glanced around nervously, then quickly ducked out of sight.

"I wonder why he's acting so strange," Nancy said.

CHAPTER 6

"Jonathan is turning me into a complete airhead," Stephanie grumbled happily as she raced back upstairs to her dorm room to get her purse.

When she had dressed for work that morning, she had been so busy daydreaming about Jonathan that she forgot her bag.

The phone was ringing as she walked into her room. "Not now!" she wailed, grabbing the receiver.

"Who is it?" she shouted into the phone.

"Stephanie?"

Stephanie drew her breath in sharply. "Dad?" A torrent of emotion washed over her—pain, anger, annoyance, love, fear. "You okay?" she asked quickly. They hadn't talked much since they'd had a blowout a few weeks ago when he canceled most of her credit cards.

71

"Better than ever," R. J. Keats said, and Stephanie relaxed.

"So?" she said. "Why are you calling?"

"Do I need a reason?"

Stephanie pursed her lips. "I guess not, but if there's nothing important, I have to get going. I'll be late for *work*." She spat out the last word. In spite of meeting Jonathan at Berrigan's, Stephanie still hated her father, or more precisely her father's new wife, Kiki, for making her have to work there.

"You're still working at that department store? Good," he said. "Steph, I like how you've taken this money situation in hand." The note of pride in her father's voice cut through her anger.

"Actually," she conceded, her own tone softening, "it's not so bad. And I met a guy there."

"Oh?" Her father chuckled softly. "He must be pretty special."

"Why do you say that?" Stephanie asked, guarded.

"Your voice," he replied. "You sound like you might be in love."

"I do?" Stephanie felt flustered. Did it show, even in her voice? "Oh, I don't know him very well yet," Stephanie protested.

"I hope it works out," he said, and Stephanie smiled. "You sound happy. Like I am with Kiki."

Stephanie's smile froze on her face. Like you are with Kiki? What a disgusting idea, she thought.

"Look, Dad, I barely know him. Get it? Don't

make a big deal out of this—and believe me, when I fall in love, it won't be at all like you and Kiki!"

"Stephanie—"

Stephanie slammed the phone down and charged out of her room. After banging the door closed behind her, she raced down the stairs.

How dare he compare what she felt for Jonathan with what he felt for Kiki? If what her dad had with Kiki was true love, Stephanie would avoid it at all costs.

"Three . . . two . . . one," Montana whispered as she kept one eye on the second hand of the KWDR clock. "Now!" She motioned to Nikki with one hand.

Nikki bit her lip and flicked the switch. The on-air light lit up, and Kara gasped. "We're on the air? Really?" She tapped the microphone.

"Yes!" Montana cried.

Kara groaned softly and buried her face in her hands.

Montana leaned into the microphone and announced in a bright voice. "Good morning, everyone out there in KWDR land . . ."

"Pssst!" Nikki whispered. "It's not morning!"

"Oh!" Montana clamped her hand over her mike, then cleared her throat. "Whoops, sorry, guys. As one of my cohosts for today's *Let's Talk*, Nikki Bennett, just pointed out . . ." Montana trained her big blue eyes on Nikki. "Oh, say hello to everyone in radio land, Nikki."

"Hi, everyone out there!" Nikki squeaked.

Montana's smile tightened. "As I was saying, Nikki kindly pointed out it's really afternoon. But who's to tell the difference on a Saturday, especially on the first Saturday after an exam week? Whoever didn't head off for the long weekend was probably partying like crazy last night, putting the word 'wild' back in Wilder."

Kara burst out laughing. "Way to go, Montana."

Montana's smile relaxed a little. She winked at Kara and pulled her mike closer. "Nikki Bennett, Kara Verbeck, and I—Montana Smith—are sitting in today for Patrice."

Kara suddenly wailed into her mike. "Oh, no! We forgot station identification."

"What do we do?" Nikki cried. "Turn everything off and start again?"

Kara saw Montana gesturing wildly at the on-air sign. Kara thought quickly and spoke into her mike. "You listeners must think we're crazy. We aren't. Or at least not totally."

Montana broke up. The sound of her laughter made Kara double over in hysterics. Kara finally managed to say, "Well, maybe we are crazy, but we're going to sort of rewind the show and begin again," Kara smiled into the mike and announced the call letters, then the time. "Anything else, Nikki?" she asked.

"Yes, the topic of the day," Nikki reminded, elbowing Montana.

Montana hemmed and hawed. "To tell you listeners the truth, we were just discussing exactly what the topic of the day should be. Kara, what are your thoughts on the matter?"

"Montana Smith!" Kara shrieked. "How can you put me on the spot like this?"

"Kara likes to complain, folks." Montana laughed. "But she's known for being able to pull rabbits out of hats."

Kara thought hard, but she seemed to have forgotten every topic she'd come up with before. Kara Verbeck, she asked herself in a panic, what do you usually like to talk about?

"Guys!" she blurted into the mike.

"Guys?" Montana and Nikki both sounded startled.

"Yes. What do *you* out there in the Wilder listening audience look for in the perfect guy or girl?"

To Kara's relief, Montana's face lit up. She picked up Kara's idea and ran with it. "Perfect!" she said breezily. "Nikki, why don't you tell us what you think makes the perfect guy?"

"Biceps!"

"No way," Kara countered.

"Why not?" Montana challenged. "If a guy is blond with biceps and a gorgeous smile, hey, that dude's for me."

"Enough about what *we* like. What about you *guys?*" Kara asked. "We know you're listening. What drives you perfectly wild about Wilder women?"

The words were no sooner out of her mouth

than the phones began to light up. "Let's take our first call."

"Kara Verbeck, is that you?"

Kara flinched as she heard Tim Downing's voice. "Hi there, Tim."

"Well, I just want to tell your audience that you drive me totally wild. You're the best."

Kara blushed. "Thanks, Tim."

Montana picked up the next call. "My name's Cindy," the caller said. "I think all of you are just great. Usually this show puts me to sleep, but I've never laughed so hard as today."

"Thanks, Cindy," Nikki said, "but you haven't answered the real question."

"I don't know," Cindy replied. "I think the perfect guy would be a mind reader."

"A psychic?" Montana joked.

"Of course not," Nikki broke in. "Cindy means someone who doesn't need everything spelled out for him. Like he'd know that when you say it doesn't matter where you go for dinner, that you really mean someplace special, like Les Peches."

"Have a heart, Nikki," Kara interjected. "Not every guy can afford a place like that."

"But maybe a dream date should be able to take you to the best place in town," Montana drawled.

All four phones lit up at once. "My name's Bill, and I think that's disgusting."

"What? That girls might want you only for your money?" Montana chided. "Or your biceps," she added.

"Ah, my biceps, now that's another matter."
Bill chuckled. "If this were TV—"

"But it's not, Bill," Kara cut in, "and there
are other callers on the line. Thanks for phoning
in, though."

Phones rang endlessly. Witty remarks spilled
out of Kara's lips. Faster, funnier, slicker than she
ever imagined she could be, even in her wildest
dreams. Everything moved so quickly that before
Kara knew it, the hour-long show was over.

Montana flipped the switch to take them off
the air. The three women got up, to make way
for the afternoon DJ.

As they left the radio station, Kara was smiling
so hard her face ached. "We did it!" she cheered.
Then she, Nikki, and Montana came together in
a big hug.

"It was great!" Nikki shouted.

"Thanks to you, Kara," Montana said gener-
ously. "That topic really hit the right note."

Kara gave a little bow, then pumped her fist in
the air. "Thanks, but it took all of us. And I've
just had the most fun I've ever had in my life!"

"What do you mean, strange? Nancy, what are
you thinking?" asked Jake, following her gaze as
she watched Nick's uncle Ed disappear through
a service entrance to his music store.

"I'm not sure," Nancy said slowly.

Jake looked hard at Nancy. "I think I know
where you're headed with all this. You can't really

believe that Nick's uncle had something to do with the tapes that are missing from your car?"

"Jake, I know you don't want to think Ed would break into my car—"

"Ed did not break into your car," Jake stated emphatically. "Why would a guy who runs a record store steal a couple of tapes from your car?"

Nancy began to look doubtful. "I know, it doesn't make sense. But he *was* carrying some tapes just now and acting very nervous. And he was also standing there in the store when that guy asked Nick for the Cybersounds' new tape. The one the TV show said was counterfeit," she said. "Nick's uncle looked uncomfortable when he told the kid he must be mistaken, that the tape had never been for sale in his store. Maybe it was. Maybe he's selling them under the counter or something." Nancy sighed.

"That's stretching it, Nancy." Jake was sure she was wrong. "Besides," he added, "how would Ed know what your car even looked like, let alone where it was parked?" Jake waved around the crowded parking lot.

"Nick knows my car," Nancy stated.

Jake stared at Nancy a moment, then began to laugh. "You're losing it for sure, Nancy Drew. Nick is one of the most honest people I've ever met. And I'm sure he and any relative of his are not into selling counterfeit tapes."

Nancy's shoulders sagged. "I don't want to believe it, either, Jake," she replied. "But first of all, my car *has* been broken into. The tapes just didn't vanish into thin air. And why was Ed in the parking lot? What was he carrying in that box?"

"How do I know?" Jake retorted. "Maybe he'd just helped a customer with something." Jake shrugged. "Who knows why he was in the lot just now? And who cares what was in the box? The guy's running a store. It could have been anything," he said in an exasperated tone of voice. "But I think it's a pretty big leap to say he came out here to break into your car. Give me a break, Nancy. How would he know you had counterfeit tapes in your car? Nick doesn't even know about the mix-up with the duffel."

Nancy nodded slowly. "That's true." She leaned back against the car and looked back toward the mall's service entrance. "I guess I am jumping to conclusions."

Jake thought back to that morning. When they had come out of the house, he and Nancy were preoccupied talking about Nancy's problems with Avery.

"Besides," he said, "back at the house, didn't you say you thought you had locked your car last night?"

Nancy looked up quickly. "Yes . . ."

"But the door was unlocked this morning, wasn't it?"

Nancy nodded. "Yes, someone may have broken into the car last night."

"That's a better possibility than someone breaking in here, in broad daylight."

"I was distracted back at the house, but I would have noticed the chipped paint around the lock, wouldn't I?" Nancy asked.

"Maybe not. And as you said before, neither of us even tried to play the tapes or looked for them when we left the house. We talked the whole way here," Jake reminded her.

"That's true. You're probably right, Jake," Nancy conceded, but Jake could tell by the tone of her voice that she wasn't convinced.

Nancy tossed her shopping bags in the backseat. "I'd still like to talk to Nick about that Cybersounds tape. Ask him outright if he knows anything." Nancy glanced at the store, then checked her watch. "But not now. We're supposed to meet Bess in ten minutes at her house for lunch."

Jake shook his head. "You won't let this go until you've talked to Nick, I guess. Well, it can't hurt," he admitted. "As long as you don't out-and-out accuse his uncle of anything." As Nancy turned on the ignition, Jake added, "In any case, we'll be seeing him tonight."

Nancy looked across the seat at Jake. "We will?"

"I asked him to join us at the club after dinner. The store will be closed by then, and he said he'd like to hang out awhile and let loose. You can clear the air with him then."

"Good," Nancy said. "A couple of answers will put my mind at rest. I promise, Jake." She reached across the seat and touched his wrist.

He knew she was apologizing, but Jake was

still annoyed at her. As smart and wonderful as Nancy was, this time Jake was sure she was way off-base. Neither Nick nor his uncle was involved in selling illegal tapes. He was certain of it.

As Ray finished singing, he drew out the last word of the ballad a full measure. Then he lifted his hand and signaled his group to close in unison. The final chord vibrated through the recording studio.

The musicians stood silent for a couple of seconds until the last bit of music died away and the engineer's voice in their headsets told them tapes were off.

"Outta sight, Ray!" Spider thumped Ray on the shoulder.

Ray took off his headset and ran his hands through his short dark hair. Singing that song always drained him. He and Ginny had written it together soon after they met. When he sang it as well as he did today, from the bottom of his heart and soul, it took even more out of him.

"Good show, guys," Ray turned around to congratulate the other members of his band.

Ray stepped out of the sound room into the studio and saw Joel Hoffman.

"Nice job," Joel mumbled, then checked his watch. "Roger, could you take the guys to lunch?"

"Aren't you joining us?" Spider asked.

"Not now. See you later." With that, Joel disappeared into one of the offices.

"Why isn't he coming along?" Ray asked

Roger as they all filed through the reception area to get their coats.

"He has some phone calls to make," Roger said quickly.

Ray noticed Roger was avoiding his eyes.

Ray shared a quick glance with Spider. "What's up?" he mouthed.

Spider blinked. "I don't know," he muttered under his breath.

Ray wanted to believe Roger's answer about Joel. But halfway through the meal, Ray was sure something was terribly wrong. Though the rest of the Beat Poets were talking a blue streak about the morning's session, Roger had barely said a word. Ray hadn't known Roger long, but whenever he spent time with the band, he tended to monopolize the conversation. He was a loud, talkative man.

"Roger," Ray started, finally working up the nerve to ask him what was going on. "I think we really performed great today."

Roger looked up from his coffee. "It went well," he said instantly.

"Then what's wrong?" Ray demanded to know.

Roger cleared his throat. "Pacific Records—they've got an idea for this band. A certain image they want to project."

"They have an image?" Ray repeated with a tight laugh.

"Yeah. You know, Ray, image is a really big part of the rock business. Anyway, they . . ." Roger heaved a sigh, then blurted out, "They love Spider's style and his look—the long-haired backroom rocker look. Ray, you don't have the right look. You're a great musician, you write great music, and you'd continue to be central to the band, but Spider's got to take over as lead singer. Be the Beat Poets' front man. He's got a more current hard-rock sound and the looks to go with it."

Ray's jaw dropped. He stared at Roger, waiting for him to say this was some kind of joke. Roger leveled his gaze at Ray and shrugged. "You've got a good voice, too, but it's more of a bluesy-country sound. Pacific Records has decided to promote the Beat Poets as a hard-rock band."

"Did you hear that?" Ray glanced from Denny to Sam to Bruce. They looked as shocked as Ray.

Finally, Ray turned to Spider sitting next to him in the booth. Spider's face was hard to read. "This is heavy, man," Spider said to Ray.

Bolstered by knowing his band would back him, Ray stated firmly, "Sorry, Roger. That's not going to happen." Ray got up and pushed back his chair. "I'm the lead singer, and the Beat Poets is my band. We play it my way or we don't play it at all. If you don't like it, we'll find a new manager. One who's willing to stick his neck out and fight for us with Pacific Records. Right, guys?" Ray turned to his band.

They were all nodding, though no one said a word.

CHAPTER 7

All week long Bess had gotten into the habit of watching TV soap operas. Actually, she watched practically anything. Focusing on the make-believe world of TV characters helped her not to think about her own life.

Ned Nickerson had come by late that morning while Bess was watching another show. Ned's visit certainly had been a surprise. She had been glad to see him and a little bit curious about how he was doing without Nancy.

He seemed fine. So much for constant, eternal love, Bess thought glumly now as she sat curled in a chair in the living room, staring at the screen. But she wasn't taking anything in. She was still thinking about Ned. He had been sympathetic about Paul and worried about her. Still, he didn't understand when she said she really wasn't up to dinner with the crowd that night.

Just when the show broke for a commercial, her doorbell rang. "Who now?" Bess grumbled.

She opened the door. "Nancy, Jake?"

"Don't look so surprised," Nancy said, walking into the hall. "We planned to have lunch together."

Bess shook her head. "I forgot. I'm sorry."

"Well, we brought you a feast," Jake announced as he followed Nancy to the kitchen.

Bess trailed behind them. "Thanks," she said.

"We stopped at that new gourmet place."

"Oh." Bess stared as Nancy took container after container out of a plastic shopping bag. She didn't feel in the mood for lunch. "You bought out the store."

"Practically," Jake admitted with a laugh.

"Should we eat here?" Nancy asked, pulling a stool up to the counter.

"Um—sure," Bess said, joining them.

"You won't believe what's been going on," Nancy said, heaping assorted cold cuts and pasta salad on a plate and putting it in front of Bess.

"Oh, what?" Bess said, trying to sound interested.

But Nancy didn't need much encouragement. "Remember what we heard on the news last night, about counterfeit tapes?"

Bess didn't, but Nancy plunged on before Bess could say a thing.

Between bites of food, Nancy and Jake were

taking turns telling some complicated story about a rock band, counterfeit tapes, Jake's lost duffel bag, and a music shop at the new mall. Bess frankly couldn't follow the story or get the connection. Soon her head began to ache from just trying to focus on all the details.

Finally, she couldn't stand it anymore. "Hey, guys, I really appreciate what you're trying to do here—keep me company and all," Bess mumbled. "But to tell you the truth, I'm tired and not very hungry, and my arm aches."

Nancy jumped up. "Oh, Bess," she cried, gathering up the food. "Why didn't you say so earlier?"

Bess shrugged. "I need to lie down."

"We're leaving now." Jake went to the sink and began rinsing the dishes. Bess stopped him. She wanted to be alone. "Don't bother. Really. My mom will deal with those later. But thanks for lunch, and thanks for asking me to join you guys tonight. Ned came by earlier and also invited me, but I can't make it."

Bess walked them to the door. Nancy turned and hugged Bess. She could tell Nancy wanted her to say something, but Bess just couldn't.

After they left, Bess was switching the TV back on when the phone rang.

"Hi," she said listlessly into the receiver.

"Bess? It's me, Holly."

"Holly Thornton?" Bess was surprised. She hadn't heard from her Kappa sister since she'd come back to River Heights.

"Yes, I thought I'd call."

"I'm glad you did," Bess said, trying to sound as if she meant it. She muted the sound on the TV with the remote but kept her eye on the screen. "So, what's up at Kappa?" she asked.

"You wouldn't believe what's going on here—"

Bess smiled. "What's Soozie Beckerman up to now?"

"How'd you guess Soozie had something to do with it? Anyway, remember that Alpha Delt guy that she met? Well . . ."

Bess tried to follow Holly's story. It was no use. She had no more luck pretending to be interested in Holly's gossip than she did in Nancy's story of counterfeit tapes. She said "Yes" and "Really" at moments she hoped were appropriate, but soon she could hear that her lack of enthusiasm had become apparent to Holly.

"Well, Bess, I think I'm wearing you out with all this stuff," Holly said, sounding a little unsure of herself.

Bess bit her lip. "I'm sorry. I was just about to take a nap when you called."

"Why didn't you say so?" Holly paused. "Hey, Bess, we really miss you here. Life at Wilder's not the same without you, you know."

Life at Wilder without Paul won't be the same for me! Bess thought. "Thanks for that, Holly. I miss everyone, too," she said dully, then hung up.

Bess sat with the phone in her lap, staring at the silent TV screen. She wondered if maybe her parents were right, that talking to some kind of counselor would help her. She had to get over this.

Get over Paul, a horrified voice inside her repeated. I don't want to get over him. I don't want to forget him. Didn't anyone understand that? I'm not ready for it. Maybe I'll never be.

Bess flicked the remote at the TV and turned on the sound. It felt better to be numb in front of the TV, better than having to think about anything.

"Knock, knock!" George said as she poked her head into Nancy's room late that afternoon.

"Oh, I didn't hear you guys come in. Did Jake pick you guys up?" Nancy asked.

"Yeah," George said, unzipping her jacket and checking her makeup in Nancy's mirror. "Now he's on the phone downstairs. The smell of Hannah's cookies baking has lured Will into the kitchen. The guys can keep themselves busy for a few minutes."

"I'll be ready in a minute," Nancy said, slipping a slinky blue dress over her head. The material sort of shimmered, and the short skirt, low-cut neck, and long sleeves showed off Nancy's figure perfectly.

"That's new," George said, nodding approval.

"Like it?"

"It's great, perfect for the Warehouse. And Jake will love it," George said as she adjusted the wide neckline of her own soft gray shirt.

"Did you hear? Ned went to see Bess," Nancy said. "But she won't come with us tonight."

George nodded. "I'm not surprised. I don't know that I'd want to go to a club so soon after what happened, and she does have a broken arm. But still, Nancy, I think she's in trouble."

"You've noticed, too?" Nancy sat down next to George and pulled a brush through her thick hair.

"What really has me worried is that she'd rather stay glued to the TV than spend time talking with any of us. I'd feel better if she were crying, or angry, or something . . ."

"If she were more like Bess," Nancy said.

"I guess TV's a way of avoiding her own life right now," George said. "I was hoping we'd get here and she'd want to see us. Instead, I'm even afraid to hug her."

"It's like she's wearing a giant hands-off sign," Nancy added.

"Maybe we should just ignore it," George said. "Let's just go over there sometime this weekend and have it out with her. Tell her she's pushing us away. Confront her."

"Really?" Nancy looked skeptical.

"Really. I think Bess needs to face up to the fact that she's burying her feelings. Hiding from them. She's going to make herself worse this way."

Nancy nodded.

After a moment she asked George, "How's your family taking to Will?"

"Super," she said with a grin. She let out a big, happy sigh. "Couldn't ask for anything better. He and my dad keep having these intense heart-to-hearts about the environment."

"That's great."

George heard the wistful note in Nancy's voice. "So?"

"So what?"

"So what's wrong here?" George closed the door to Nancy's room and lowered her voice. "You can't tell me your dad doesn't like Jake. Last night everyone seemed so buddy-buddy."

"Oh, that's not the problem." Nancy's laugh was bitter. "Everyone likes Jake. Jake likes everyone."

"But?"

Nancy leaned against the windowsill next to George. She folded her arms across her chest and stared at her feet. "Oh, George!" she exclaimed. "It's me."

"You and Jake?" George couldn't believe it.

Nancy shook her head quickly. "No. Jake and I are fine. Just fine." She eyed George. "Me and Avery."

George blinked. "Am I hearing right? You loved Avery at first sight and have been singing her praises since you met her. Suddenly you don't like her?"

"Doesn't make sense, does it?" Nancy sounded miserable. George watched her go over to her closet and poke around for some shoes. A moment later Nancy turned around. "It's just that she's changing everything."

George considered that a moment. "Everything's bound to change now that your dad is seeing someone, Nancy."

"I don't mean that kind of change. I mean," Nancy blurted, "she's redecorating, and Dad's letting her."

"Redecorating?" George let that sink in. She studied Nancy's room. "The whole house?"

"I don't know." Nancy dropped down heavily in a chair and put on a pair of heels. "But she's starting with Dad's study."

"Oh." George wasn't sure what to say. "But she's not doing your room, is she?"

"She'd better not!" Nancy sounded vehement.

"I guess so!" George said, amazed at Nancy's passion. "Hey, Nancy, everything will work out, with time."

"Right." But Nancy's scowl told George that Nancy wasn't convinced.

Back at the recording studio after lunch, the atmosphere felt about as cheerful as that at a funeral home.

Ray's musicians sat around the small reception area, talking in low hushed voices, while Ray paced the floor.

Every so often he glanced up at the door marked Office. Roger Hall and Joel Hoffman had been locked inside for almost an hour, deciding his future *and* the future of the Beat Poets, the band he had fought to shape, hold together, and turn into a tight, successful act. The Beat Poets was Ray's baby, and part of him would live or die with it.

Ray wanted to believe that Roger had really listened to him back at the restaurant. That he was fighting to keep Ray as lead singer in the band—which, as far as Ray was concerned, translated into making Pacific Records honor their deal with the Beat Poets.

"Ray, sit down," Spider said.

"I can't." Ray continued to pace. "I mean, where do they get off with this . . ." he started to say, when at last the office door swung open. Ray's mouth went dry. Roger Hall was standing in the doorway, poker-faced.

"Come on in, Ray," Roger said.

Ray squared his shoulders and marched right past his band. Without a backward glance, he knew that they were behind him one hundred percent.

Roger closed the door behind Ray. "Sit down," he said, motioning to one of two chairs in front of a large wooden desk. Joel sat behind the desk, looking Ray over. He smiled at Ray.

Ray didn't smile back. "So?" he said.

"Ray," Joel began, "I'm not sure Roger made things clear over lunch. So I'll spell them out for you now." Joel leaned forward. "Pacific Records is one of the top labels in the business, and when it comes to packaging a band commercially we have a bit more experience than you do."

Ray definitely didn't like where this conversation seemed to be going. He sat perfectly still and tried to keep all expression off his face. But inside he was seething—and was very scared.

"As Joel says," Roger interjected, "Pacific knows the market. They think the Beat Poets is a good band with a potentially killer sound. Pacific can send you guys to the top of the charts."

"If you play the game our way."

"Hey, man, this is no game. Music's my life," Ray countered passionately.

"Don't be such a hothead," Joel warned, a steely note in his voice. "We want to work with you, but on our terms."

"Which are?"

"Spider becomes the band's front man and lead singer," Joel said.

Ray stared at Joel dumbfounded. He turned to Roger. "I thought you were supposed to be on my side!" he cried.

"I'm on the side of the Beat Poets. I don't represent you individually, Ray," Roger said tightly.

Ray jumped up. "Well, *I* am the Beat Poets. They're my band, and I'm the lead singer, period. What I say goes."

"You're under contract to us," Joel said evenly. "If you don't go along with this, you're fired."

"Fired?" Ray jumped up. "That's crazy, man. You can't fire me."

"Yes, we can," Joel said, standing up and glancing at his watch. "Read the contract."

Ray looked at Roger, who averted his gaze. Ray knew in a flash that Roger wasn't in his corner at all. He was out for himself on this one. He wasn't going to jeopardize his relationship with Pacific Records for Ray.

"I'll tell you what," Joel said, picking up the phone. Before he dialed he continued, "Think about it for a couple of days. Hash it out with the guys. Maybe you'll come around to seeing it our way. Meanwhile, the session's over for now. I'm not going to waste more tape and studio time on rehearsing cuts we can't use with you singing lead."

"We don't need to hash anything out." Ray was adamant.

"Maybe not," Joel said sharply. "But you're under contract to us now—the whole band is—and you'd better read that contract. *All* of it, Ray. Maybe then you'll change your mind. Not being the front man isn't so bad considering the alternative—having no music career at all."

"You can't threaten me," Ray challenged. Then he banged out of the room. "Come on, guys, we're packing up and heading out of this place. Now."

"But what about our contract?" Spider asked.

"We'll talk about that back in Weston. I want to study it first." Ray couldn't believe how determined and angry he managed to sound, when his insides were turning to Jell-O.

Joel Hoffman and Roger Hall were very slick. Ray had a sick, terrible feeling as he grabbed his guitar and led the way out of the studio. Pacific Records had decided to play hardball, and he was a dumb kid who didn't know the rules of the game.

When Nancy and George walked into the living room, Jake, Will, Carson Drew and Avery seemed to be deep in conversation. Nancy noticed Jake's eyebrows lift in appreciation as he took in her new dress. When he looks at me it always makes my heart flip-flop, she thought, smiling at him.

Then Nancy caught Avery's eye. She hadn't seen Avery since breakfast. Avery's smile was tentative; her usually open expression seemed wary, cautious.

Nancy managed a weak smile back. She suddenly felt awfully silly about her blowup that morning. As she settled down next to Jake on the sofa, she resolved to be extra nice to Avery from then on.

"Nancy, Jake's been telling us about the counterfeit tapes," Carson Drew said.

"What counterfeit tapes?" George asked.

Nancy explained quickly and was surprised when Will and George exchanged a quick glance. "You knew about them?" Nancy asked Will.

"No. Not until now, but yesterday we ran into Kate Terrell and Jeff Rayburn at Keelor Falls."

George jumped in. "I mentioned the mix-up

with Jake's duffel bag, and when I asked Jeff if he knew of someone else selling tapes at the festival, he acted weird."

"I thought he was just being uptight about something," Will declared. "But maybe it was the mention of the bag of tapes. He might have known they were counterfeit."

"Now, that's interesting," Nancy pondered out loud. It might all be a coincidence, but the counterfeit tapes did have some connection with someone at Wilder, since they turned up in a duffel bag in Thayer Hall. Maybe Jeff wasn't involved, but then again, maybe . . .

"You know, I called my apartment just now." Jake interrupted her chain of thought. "And Dennis answered. He's one of my roommates," Jake explained to Nancy's father and Avery. "He told me that someone had called earlier and said it was really important to get in touch with me."

"Maybe someone found *your* duffel bag," Avery suggested.

"Hey, yeah," Jake said. "That's a possibility. The caller could be the owner of the other duffel."

"And those counterfeit tapes," Carson Drew mused.

Jake nodded. "Dennis gave him your name and number."

"It was a guy?" Nancy asked.

"Yes," Jake answered. "But now, after hearing about Kate and Jeff, I wonder if that guy could have been Jeff."

"He's in the area," George reminded them.

Nancy frowned. "It could just as easily be someone else."

"Whoever called my place could have looked up the Drews in the phone book and found the street address," Jake added, finishing Nancy's thought. "Then he could have come and broken into your car, Nancy, to retrieve those tapes. The ones we left in the car were right out in plain sight."

"You might be right," Carson Drew said, "but what worries me is that all he found were a couple of the tapes. What if he comes back for the bag and the rest of them?"

"Good point, Dad," Nancy said. "I thought about that. If he knows someone is onto him, he'll want to get the rest of the tapes."

"I'm taking that bag," her dad said, retrieving it from the front hall under the coatrack as he spoke. "And I'm locking it in my study in case he comes snooping around the house."

"Meanwhile," Avery said, "I think you kids should forget about the whole thing for tonight. Go to the Warehouse and have fun."

"Good thinking," Jake said. They walked out to the driveway. As they all climbed into Nancy's car, she suddenly had an idea.

"What are you guys doing tomorrow?" Nancy asked Will and George.

"We're loose," Will said.

"I'm pretty sure whoever belongs to that duffel bag intended to sell those tapes at the Keelor

Falls Festival tomorrow," Nancy said, backing out of the driveway. "Why don't we go to the festival? We can check out the vendors and see who besides Jeff and Kate is selling tapes."

"Great idea," Will replied.

George cleared her throat. "I'd love to go, but I want to spend some time with Bess."

"Let's call and ask her to come along. Maybe being outdoors will help her," Nancy said. "She loves crafts fairs. Even if we learn nothing about the tapes, we're bound to have a good time." Then, suddenly remembering Kate's earrings, Nancy smiled to herself. A pair of handcrafted hoops would make the perfect peace offering for her to give to Avery.

CHAPTER 8

Saturday night at Anthony's Café, Kara was having the time of her life. "I never want this day to end!" she yelled to Tim, Nikki, and Montana over the strains of the jukebox. That afternoon's radio stint had left Kara feeling fantastic, and she wanted to spread her happiness around.

Kara grinned at the student waiter as he deposited a frothy drink in front of her. "If I were a millionaire," she told him, "I'd give you a semester's worth of tuition as a tip."

The waiter cocked his head at the sound of Kara's voice. "Hey, I know your voice. Aren't you one of those crazy women who was on *Let's Talk* today?"

"We all are," Montana said with a big smile.

"In person," Nikki added, elbowing Kara.

"Cool!" he said. "This round's on me."

Kara, Montana, and Nikki gaped at him.

"We're stars!" Nikki cried.

"Do you realize what this means?" Tim asked. "You're famous on campus."

"Oh, Tim, do you really think so?" Kara believed him for half a second. Then she laughed. "Of course you don't." Kara's mood flattened ever so slightly.

"What's this about fame?" Ginny Yuen asked, pulling a chair up to their table. "I'm not sure I want to be suitemates with another star."

"I would. I'd love it!" Liz Bader exclaimed, squeezing in between Ginny and Kara. "Almost as much as I loved your show this afternoon. You three were too much!"

"That's a compliment, girls," Stephanie Keats drawled as she walked up to the table.

"Hi, Steph," Kara greeted her suitemate. Though Stephanie seemed her usual edgy self, her eyes glowed. Then Kara spotted Jonathan Bauer. She'd only met him once before, but he seemed to be a nice person.

Stephanie propped herself against the wall near the table and looked down at Kara. "Actually, you three surprised me today."

"You really listened to us?" Montana asked.

To Kara's surprise, Stephanie said, "I did. During my break at the store. I caught only part of the show." Stephanie shrugged. "I expected you to blow it. Instead"—she smiled broadly—"I thought it was fun. Not like everything else on that stupid station."

"Steph," Jonathan interrupted, "there's a free table."

" 'Bye." Stephanie waved breezily as she started for the table. "And I, for one, girls, wouldn't mind hearing you take over for that dreary Patrice what's-her-name again."

"I don't believe it," Liz murmured. "Was that Stephanie Keats or a clone missing her sarcasm gene?"

Ginny was thoughtful. "It's Stephanie, and I'm beginning to think the rumors of love changing her are not exaggerated."

Kara was fascinated. She stared past Tim's shoulder at Stephanie and Jonathan. They were sitting very close together at a table in the corner. It didn't take a brain surgeon to figure out that they were heavily involved with each other already, though she was sure they hadn't been dating long. Love, Kara thought, really does work miracles.

"Hi. Are you three the girls from the *Let's Talk* show today?"

At the sound of the deep voice, Kara looked up. A handsome guy she'd never seen before was standing in front of her. She nodded.

"I'm on the track and field team, and we had a blast listening to you during lunch break."

"No kidding?" Montana gasped.

"My buddies and I were wondering if we could buy you coffee," the guy said.

Kara met Tim's glance. He'd tilted back his

chair and was looking on with an amused expression.

Kara cracked a smile. Tim was being such a good sport about all this. "Sure," she said.

"And when," asked the guy, "are you three going to be on *Let's Talk* again?"

Kara heaved a sigh and glanced at Montana. Montana shrugged. "It was a one-shot deal," she said.

"Oh, that's too bad," he said.

"Yeah," Kara remarked, her spirits falling. "We did our time. Unless there's a miracle, we've had our fifteen minutes of fame."

Strobe lights flickered in the cavernous room of the Warehouse. The sound system was cranked up full volume, as the wooden floor boards vibrated to the insistent bass of the dance music. Jake stood enjoying the music and soaking it all in.

"River Heights sure has some surprises!" he shouted to Nancy. "This is a great club."

"It's pretty new," Nancy informed him. He bent down to hear her voice over the music. Nancy deposited a light, feathery kiss on his ear, and Jake felt a rush of emotion. Nancy had been running hot and cold all weekend. He was sure it all had to do with Bess or whatever was bothering her about Avery. Still, he hated it when Nancy was being distant.

"So you don't have a history of lots of heavy dates here?" he asked, leaning against her.

Nancy rolled her eyes. "Hey, what's past is past—for *both* of us."

Jake smiled. Nancy and he both had had heavy-duty relationships before they'd met each other. Whoever he'd loved before Nancy didn't matter to him now. She was telling him she felt the same.

"Let's grab that table in the corner," Will said.

"Hey," George said. "I thought we were going to dance."

"Me, too," Jake said. As soon as they ordered sodas, Jake was on his feet, pulling Nancy onto the dance floor.

"*This* is what I really needed," Nancy said.

"The perfect way to shake away all the school blues," Jake joked, unable to take his eyes off Nancy. Right then she looked particularly beautiful—the blue of her dress matched her big eyes, and her red-blond hair glistened in the light.

After a few fast songs, the lights dimmed, and a slow tune came on. As they swayed to the rhythm of the love song, Jake felt as if he were riding the crest of a great, wonderful wave. Being this close to Nancy always gave him a heady feeling.

Jake buried his face in Nancy's hair, breathing in the clean, fresh scent of her shampoo. Suddenly he felt her body stiffen. He pulled back to look at her. She was staring toward the entrance. Jake followed her gaze.

Nancy's old boyfriend, Ned, was standing in the door, watching them dance. Ned's presence was obviously making Nancy feel weird. Jake tightened his arms around her waist, but Nancy was still a little stiff. After a few seconds she stopped moving and leaned back from him. "Hey," she said, her voice slightly strained. "Look who just walked in. It's Ned. Let's go over and show him to our table."

Jake noticed the bright, false-sounding note in Nancy's voice. "All right," he said, his jaw tight.

Ned was all smiles as they walked up. "Hi, Jake," he said.

"Ned," Jake said. "So how are things?"

"Okay." Then Ned shifted his gaze to Nancy. "Nice dress. Haven't been here since we—when did it open, Nan?"

"August," Nancy said, leading the way back to their table.

"I don't remember it being this big. You should have seen this dump before they renovated it," Ned said to Jake.

"Really," Jake replied, trying to sound interested and not jealous. So Nancy had danced with Ned here the way she'd been dancing with him now. He realized what he was thinking and hated himself for thinking it.

"Ned!" George jumped up from the table and threw herself into Ned's arms. "Oh, have I missed you." Jake watched as George introduced Will to Ned.

"Ned, I hear you went to see Bess today," Nancy said.

Jake watched Nancy carefully as she talked

with Ned about Bess. Her eyes shone as she gazed up at Ned. A feeling stirred in Jake's gut: jealousy—real green, nasty stuff.

Before he could tell himself there was nothing to be jealous about, Will said, "Jake, here comes Nick. This is turning into a real party."

Jake glanced over his shoulder. Nick was coming across the floor, nimbly skirting the dancers. Jake was never so happy to see anyone in his life.

"Nick!" he cried, and waved. Jake pulled Nancy aside. Speaking into her ear so she'd hear him over the music, he said, "Nancy, I'm going to talk to Nick outside, about the tapes."

Nancy nodded, then turned back to the group and instantly resumed her conversation with Ned, George, and Will. She seemed more interested in talking to Ned than in checking out what was happening with the tapes and his friend.

Jake was annoyed. Nancy was the one who had first suspected Nick's uncle and maybe Nick. Now she didn't seem to care. His jaw set, he jammed his hands into his pockets and strode over to Nick.

"I need to talk to you," Jake yelled over the music, motioning toward the door.

A moment later they were in the parking lot. A chain-link fence separated the club grounds from the river. Across the river the lights of downtown River Heights twinkled. Jake leaned back against Nick's car.

"So, how did it go today at your uncle's store?" Jake opened.

Nick smiled broadly and let out a little laugh. "Great. But, for me, exhausting."

Jake glanced into the car and saw a cardboard carton full of tapes on the backseat. The bootlegged Cybersounds tape was right on top. He felt sick.

"Nick," Jake said, "why do you have that tape?" He pointed through the back windshield.

Nick came up to Jake and stood beside him. He peered into the car. "I don't know. What about it?"

"Did you know that there are pirated Cybersounds tapes being sold?"

"What?" Nick acted amazed. He indicated the tape on top of the box. "That tape?"

Jake nodded. "The one that's not supposed to be released until next week."

Jake watched Nick's face as the truth slowly dawned on him. "This is the tape that kid was asking for in the store, isn't it?"

"Yes."

Nick scratched his head. "I don't get it."

Jake waited for him to say more. Finally Jake asked, "How'd this stuff get in your car?"

"My uncle used the car this afternoon. But I don't know a thing about these tapes or any counterfeit business." Then, looking quickly up at Jake, Nick added firmly, "And Ed doesn't, either. I'm sure of that. He wouldn't be involved with anything counterfeit. Not if he knew about it."

Jake nodded. "For sure," Jake said, and hoped

he looked convinced. But as he and Nick headed back to the Warehouse, Jake wondered. Nick's story about his uncle borrowing the car seemed a little too pat, too convenient. Were Nick and Ed hiding something? Did Nick know more than he was letting on?

"So tell me, didn't you love the Warehouse?" Nancy said as she and Jake drove home. It was late, and Nancy felt up and happy still.

"It's a nice place," Jake replied.

Nice? Nancy stole a sidelong glance at Jake. He seemed content enough, but he'd been awfully quiet since they'd dropped Will and George off at the Faynes'.

"Nice," she said out loud. "Is that all you can say?"

"Cool, it was a very cool place," Jake said solemnly. A second later he chuckled, then reached across the seat and patted Nancy's hand. His touch sent a shot of warmth through her. Earlier that evening, back in the club, Ned had patted her hand the same way. Ned's touch hadn't set off any sparks. They really had become "just friends."

Jake and Ned had actually gotten along, too. They had talked to each other, and Ned really seemed to like Jake. As she replayed the events of the evening in her mind, Nancy was sure of that. Ned liked Jake. But Jake?

"You're awfully quiet," Nancy said as they approached her street.

"I'm a bit talked out," Jake said.

"You're scared Nick wasn't being up-front?" Nancy asked. Jake had shared the gist of his conversation with Nick before they dropped off Will and George. None of them knew what to make of it.

"That, too."

Hmmm, now Nancy was sure of it. Something was bothering Jake, and if it wasn't Nick, then there was only one other possibility. She couldn't imagine confident, hard-nosed Jake Collins being jealous of Ned. Still . . .

"So, what do you think about Ned?" she asked playfully.

"Nice guy, Nancy. I wouldn't expect less." Jake said tersely.

"You know, Jake, it made me really happy to see you two getting along." She pulled over to the side of the road and stopped the car. Jake looked at her questioningly.

Nancy turned and stared directly at him. "Jake, you're the guy for me," she said, and paused. "And I'm happier than I've ever been in my life since meeting you."

He reached over and kissed her hard. They pulled back and smiled at each other.

"Nancy—" Jake started, and searched her eyes. His face was so intense, his expression so happy, he took Nancy's breath away. She drew him toward her and wanted to tell him how much she loved him. But she couldn't find her voice right then. Instead she pressed her lips to his and gave herself up to another long, sweet kiss.

In Jake's arms Nancy lost track of time. She had no idea if they'd been kissing for seconds or hours, but suddenly the screech of a siren pierced the air.

"What the . . . ?" Jake said as they pulled apart. A police car roared by them.

"Hey," Nancy cried, "it looks like that police car is stopping at our end of the block." She started the car and began to drive as Jake strained to see where the trouble was.

Nancy pulled up to the Drew house as two uniformed men were getting out of the police car. "Excuse me, I live here. What's going on?" she asked, opening the car door.

"Nancy!" Her father's voice called out.

Jake had already climbed out of the car. "What happened?"

"Someone just tried to break into the house," Carson Drew said. Hannah and Avery stood next to him, wearing their robes and slippers and shivering in the night air.

Jake and Nancy shared a glance. The tapes!

CHAPTER 9

The clock on Ray's desk read 1:00 A.M. He'd been holed up in his dorm room for five or six hours now. Ever since he got back from Chicago.

He rubbed his eyes and forced himself to read Paragraph Four, Section B, Part III of the Beat Poets' Pacific Records contract again. Not that the small print would say anything different this time around.

"I've been had!" he groaned, staring at the pages spread out on his desk.

Joel Hoffman and Pacific Records really knew what they were doing when they drew up that agreement.

The crazy part was Ray had walked into the whole shabby deal with both eyes open. He *had* read the document through from start to finish before he signed it. But he'd gone over it only

110

once, skimming the hard parts, not bothering to try to understand the legal double-speak.

When he'd reached the last page and scrawled his name on the dotted line, he'd had no idea he'd signed away all control over *his* band. Supposedly the Beat Poets' manager would have kept an eye out for this sort of legal trap. Roger was a lawyer, and he must have known what rights Ray was signing away.

Roger had sworn he'd checked out every detail of the deal and urged them to sign it, fast, before Pacific changed its mind. Ray had listened to Roger, and fallen for Roger's assurances hook, line, and sinker. But he couldn't blame Roger completely. Ray could read perfectly well. If he had taken the time, he could have figured out the small print, the finer points, as he had just now.

Joel hadn't been bluffing. Pacific Records had every right in the world to fire him. It was spelled out in no uncertain terms. They reserved the right to hire and fire all band personnel. They had the right to mold the band's image in any way they deemed profitable to both parties. And there was more of the same crummy legal drivel.

It boiled down to just one thing as far as Ray was concerned. Unless he caved in and agreed to play backup to Spider Kelly as lead singer, Pacific could boot him out of his own band.

No way was he going to cave in. Even if that meant being blackballed in the music business from now on. Because that's exactly what Joel

Hoffman seemed to be threatening that afternoon in the recording studio.

Ray shut off the desk lamp and sat on the bed without taking his clothes off. He shouldn't have trusted Roger. Maybe Roger was out to promote Spider from the get-go. He was Spider's brother-in-law, after all. Maybe he had secretly maneuvered the deal with Pacific so Spider would become a big star.

Ray stared at the ceiling. He felt so stupid, so hopeless. Ginny had told him to read the contract carefully. But he'd told her not to worry—Roger was trustworthy.

Thinking of Ginny, Ray's heart ached. He should have listened to her. If only she were around. No matter how tough things got, he could see them through with Ginny by his side.

He closed his eyes, picturing her. Suddenly he sat up. Ginny *was* around this weekend. She was working at the hospital over the break. He reached for the phone and began to dial the number. Halfway through he hung up.

No. He couldn't do that. Ginny had made it clear when they ran into each other that she didn't want anything to do with him. She had definitely pulled back when he tried to touch her. They had agreed to break up, and for her the decision was final.

Whatever went down with the band and Pacific Records, Ray had to weather it alone.

Ray turned over on his side and punched his

pillow. There was no one to blame but himself if his career went down the tubes.

"Mr. Drew," said the officer, training his flashlight on the back door, "look. The burglar or burglars jimmied the lock." Nancy followed her father over to the door.

The other officer came back from searching the yard. "No one's around now. Whoever tried to break in is gone."

"Were the outside lights on before the robbery?" the first officer asked Carson Drew. The cop pulled out a clipboard and began taking some notes. As she listened to the police question her father, Nancy glanced around the immediate area to see if she saw anything unusual.

"In front but not in back. I put those lights on as soon as Avery told me she heard something downstairs," Carson Drew said. "That probably sent them running. By the time we called nine-one-one, whoever had tried to break in was gone."

"Can you tell if anything was stolen?" one of the officers asked.

"It doesn't look like it, but we haven't checked everything yet," he replied. Nancy noticed he didn't say anything about the tapes.

"You do that," one of the officers suggested. "And make a list of anything you find missing. We'll add it to our report. Odd," he said, "breaking into the kitchen in the middle of the night with a car in the driveway and then rushing out without taking anything."

The police combed the yard again and searched the block, but no thief turned up. "We'll come back in the morning to check again in daylight," one of the officers told Carson Drew as he closed his notebook.

"I can't imagine why anyone would want to break into our house," Hannah said as they all walked back into the kitchen, "but I think I'll just go get the silver, and count it to see if it's all there."

Nancy shared a glance with her father and Jake.

"It's the tapes, isn't it?" Jake said after Hannah left the room.

"Pretty safe bet," Nancy replied.

"That's what I thought," Carson Drew said. "I'm going to check if the duffel bag is still in my study." He left the kitchen with Avery following him.

Nancy grabbed a flashlight and went back outside with Jake. She ran the light around the back stoop. "Look, Jake, see where the paint on the door frame is chipped?"

Jake leaned over. "They left in a rush," he said, pointing to the doormat with a wry laugh.

It had been shoved up against a big terra-cotta flower pot. As Nancy bent down to straighten the mat, something glittery caught her eye.

She brushed away the dead leaves and found

an earring. It was crafted of painted metal, and Nancy recognized it immediately.

"Jake," Nancy said, "look what I found."

"An earring?" Jake glanced down at it.

"Not just *an* earring. I saw some very much like this on Friday afternoon, outside the Wilder Student Union. Jeff and Kate were selling them."

"Jeff as in Jeff Rayburn," Jake repeated.

Nancy nodded. "Jeff might have been here. Maybe he tried to break in and find the tapes. Remember George told him about the mix-up with your duffel at Thayer Hall?" she said as they went back into the house.

"Does he know where you live?"

"No, but remember that guy who phoned your apartment back in Weston earlier? As you said, he could have looked up my address once he got my name."

"So it could be Jeff, then. Keelor Falls isn't far from here," Jake said.

"Only half an hour, at the most," Nancy told him.

Hannah was at the kitchen table counting the silverware. "Nothing's missing here," she said. "I think I'll turn in. This has all been too much for my old bones."

" 'Night Hannah," Nancy said as her father came back into the kitchen.

"Dad," Nancy asked quickly, "was the duffel bag there?"

"Yes," he said. "The door was still locked. As far as I can tell, the burglar probably never got as far as the kitchen. So far, nothing seems to be missing."

"That's a bit of good news," Nancy said, feeling only mildly relieved.

"We'll check again in the morning, before we call the police to file a final report," her dad said. "Nancy, this break-in has me concerned about the tapes. I think the police should know about them."

"But, Dad, if we take the tapes in now, with no idea who the bag belongs to, how are we going to explain how we have counterfeit tapes?" Nancy said. "I mean, it sounds pretty suspicious—Jake saying he just happened to take the wrong duffel bag, one that looked just like his. Doesn't it?"

"I suppose, but I don't like this whole situation," her dad said, frowning.

Nancy placed a hand on her father's arm. "Look, we have some ideas about who might be involved with this tape scam. Just give me a little more time. If we can't find out anything in the next day or so, we'll go to the police, okay?"

Carson Drew nodded and said, "All right. Now, I think it's about time we turned in." He and Avery said good night and went back upstairs.

Jake and Nancy sat at the counter in silence. After a moment Jake spoke up.

"That earring you found definitely seems to point to Jeff. So that takes some of the pressure off Nick," he remarked, then added reluctantly, "but maybe we shouldn't totally rule out Nick and his uncle. Remember that carton of tapes that I saw in Nick's car tonight?"

"I almost forgot about that." Nancy thought a moment. "I can't quite believe Nick would try to break into the house, though, just to get the tapes back. Besides, he was still at the club when we left."

"And this is definitely not Nick's earring," Jake said with a tight laugh.

Nancy put her arm around his shoulder. "I know you're still worried that Nick might have something to do with this."

Jake shrugged. "Yeah. I don't want to think it, but I can't shake the feeling that his uncle is somehow involved. This morning when that kid was trying to buy the Cybersounds' new tape, Ed acted like it was the first he'd heard of it. But then he put that carton in Nick's car, and the counterfeit tape was definitely there."

Nancy had a hunch he was right about Nick's uncle. Nick might not have tried to break into her house to steal the bag. But Ed's Music World was clearly involved in the Cybersounds tape scam.

"You know, Nan," Jake said, getting up and putting their cups in the dishwasher, "I thought we were going to have a laid-back, fun weekend." He leaned against the sink and flashed her a wistful smile. "The *fun* part's been a little thin."

Nancy wanted to deny it, but she couldn't. Between Bess, the Cybersounds tapes, Avery, Ned, and now the burglaries, the long break was beginning to feel like an emotional roller-coaster ride.

"I guess you're right," she said finally, walking up to him. She circled his neck with her arms and smiled into his eyes. Tracing the outline of his jaw with her finger, she said in a soft voice, "But it's not over yet. We can still make up for lost time."

Jake laughed and leaned down with his face just inches from hers. "Starting now?"

"Starting now," Nancy murmured, melting against him.

Sunday morning Ginny was halfway between the shower and her room when the phone rang. "Rats!" she exclaimed, and raced to answer it. It was very early, and Liz was still dead to the world.

Ginny managed to grab the receiver before the second ring. "Hello," she whispered into the phone.

"Ginny? Is that you?"

Recognizing the voice, Ginny grinned. "Hi, Frank." She yanked the phone cord. "Wait a minute," she whispered, stretching the cord into the hallway.

"My roommate's still sleeping." Quietly she closed the door and settled down on the floor, tucking her bare toes under the hem of her terry robe. "So, Frank," she said, "what's up?"

"I was wondering if you'd like to go to brunch today."

Ginny caught her breath. "Brunch?" she repeated slowly. "Umm." You're not ready for this, a voice inside told her. Ray was not a done deal. And even if he were, Ginny knew it would take a while before she'd be ready to go out with someone else. Frank's next words amazed her.

"Hey, Ginny, this isn't a loaded question. I know you've got a lot going on right now, between the hospital work, and classes, and"— Frank paused ever so slightly—"and Ray. I know that's not completely settled yet. But don't worry, this isn't a date sort of thing."

Ginny leaned back against the wall and smiled. "As long as you put it that way," she said cheerfully, "I'd love to go. It's always great to spend time talking with you."

"Ditto," Frank said. Ginny could actually hear him smiling. "I just would like to get to know you better as a friend."

"Me, too. So where? When?"

They agreed to meet at Java Joe's. After Frank hung up, Ginny sat on the floor, holding the phone with one hand and her bathrobe shut with the other. Suddenly she realized talking to Frank just now had made her feel good—not just good, but the best she'd felt in weeks.

As Ray sat at the Bumblebee Diner with Denny, Sam, Spider, and Bruce, his one consolation was that they all looked as miserable as he felt.

"So that's it, guys," he said, stirring sugar into

his coffee. "Pacific Records has the right to fire me if I don't go along with Spider being the lead singer. Do you believe it?"

"Lousy!" Denny exclaimed.

Sam shook his head.

Bruce looked across the table toward Spider. Ray followed his gaze. "You agree, don't you, Spider?"

"Yeah, sure." Spider heaved a sigh. "Ray, this is really a drag. Can we do anything about it?"

Ray shrugged. "No—we have to break the contract. That's it. I'm not going to let Pacific Records take over *my* band."

Denny frowned. "But, Ray, we all signed that contract. Can't they do something to us? Like sue us for breaking it?"

Ray stared at Denny. "You can't be serious."

"I don't know. . . ." Sam said slowly. "I mean, there must be legal consequences—not for you, if they fire you, but for us if we walk out."

"I don't believe I'm hearing this." Ray turned to Spider for support. What he saw on Spider's face made him feel sick. "Spider, what's going on here?"

Spider poked a fork into his pancakes. "Look, Ray, I can't imagine making music without you."

Ray could hear the *but* coming and braced himself. "What are you saying?"

"I'm saying that we don't want the Beat Poets to split up. We don't want to lose you. But if the choice is between no recording contract or me taking over the lead, we're all pretty much decided we're going to stick with Pacific Records and try to go for it."

For a moment Ray actually felt as if the floor had opened up under him.

"But what we really hope," Sam added quickly, "is that you'll change your mind. It'll still be your music we play. Your songs. You can still lead the band. You just won't be the front man."

Ray looked at his band, his friends, the people he had trusted more than anyone in the world. "And when," he asked in a quiet voice, "did you all come to this decision?" He got to his feet and jammed his fists into his pockets.

Three pairs of eyes turned to Spider, and Ray's worst suspicions were confirmed. Spider, his best friend, had really turned against him. Spider, Roger Hall's brother-in-law.

He took a step toward Spider. He forced down the urge to slug him.

Spider averted his eyes. "Last night. We got together at the garage and talked. We decided this was too big an opportunity to pass up."

Ray zipped up his jacket and stared down at the guys. His gaze traveled from Sam, to Denny, to Bruce, and finally rested on Spider. "You rotten creeps. I can't believe this. Without me you'd have no contract with Pacific. You'd have nothing."

"Ray, don't do this," Spider said.

"Shut up!" Ray shouted. Some customers at the counter turned around. Ray didn't care. "I'm not *doing* a thing. I'm the lead singer of this band—not just because I want to be the front man but because my voice is part of the sound of the Beat Poets. This is my band. I'm not going to be jerked around by any record company—or by guys I thought were my friends."

Ray tossed a five-dollar bill onto the table and stormed out of the diner. He didn't pay attention to where his feet were taking him.

In the space of a couple of weeks his whole world had collapsed—first Ginny, and now his band had deserted him. Ray felt as if someone had kicked him in the chest and knocked the heart right out of him.

CHAPTER 10

Is Bess coming to Keelor Falls with us?" Jake asked Nancy when she walked into the kitchen. It was late Sunday morning, and everyone had already eaten breakfast. Hannah was making Nancy and Jake lunch out of the remains of Saturday's deli treats.

"No, and neither are George and Will," Nancy replied, pouring herself a cup of coffee. After the burglary attempt the night before Nancy had lain awake for hours, her thoughts bouncing from Jeff, to Nick, to Bess, to Ned. She felt out of it now, and talking to Bess a few minutes ago hadn't helped.

"Why not?" Avery asked, coming in from the dining room. At the sight of her, Nancy's chest tightened. Was she ever going to get used to seeing Avery have the run of the house?

"Bess is still too depressed," Jake said.

"She's been through a lot," Carson Drew added, returning his toolbox to the closet by the back door. He'd just finished fixing the jimmied lock.

"But she's not acting like herself, Dad," Nancy said. Bess's usually enthusiastic voice sounded so dead on the phone, Nancy remembered. "When I told George that Bess had begged off, George said she'd stay and have a talk with her this afternoon. It's just too important to put off."

"Here's your lunch," Hannah said, putting the sandwiches into a cooler. "I'm afraid I made enough for Bess, Will, and George. But from what I've seen of Jake's appetite, he'll probably be able to take care of their share." She chuckled.

Carson Drew looked up from washing his hands at the sink. "Too bad you made plans to go to the festival. Avery and I wanted to spend more time with you two."

"So why don't you come with us?" Jake suggested. "Hannah already packed enough lunch."

"No!" Nancy blurted out before she had time to think about it. Behind her she heard Avery suck in her breath. Her father stopped drying his hands and just looked at her. The disappointment in his eyes sent the color rushing to her face. "Umm, it's not a good idea. Jake and I need some time alone together. . . ." Nancy started. Then she remembered she and Jake weren't supposed to be going alone at all. They'd planned to spend the day with George and Will and Bess.

"That's okay," her dad said, but Nancy could hear the hurt in his voice.

She made herself turn to face Avery and her father. "I'm sorry, Avery, Dad. I don't know what got into me. That was rotten."

"You're upset about Bess," Avery said.

"Yes, but"—Nancy made herself smile—"let's just do it. All four of us together. A kind of double date!" she said. "Besides, we can't let all this food go to waste. But if you come along, you're going to do your share of shopping!"

Her father smiled at her. "I'm game," he said.

But as Nancy went upstairs to finish dressing, she realized she didn't feel "game" at all. She didn't want to spend time with Avery.

She couldn't believe her feelings about her father's girlfriend had done such a turn-around. At Wilder, Avery had seemed so cool. At home, Nancy couldn't stand being with her.

She wasn't going to let her feelings about Avery spoil more of her weekend with Jake, though.

Besides, shopping with Avery had been fun once, maybe it would be again. If they just spent time away from the house together, things might improve, she tried to convince herself.

When George arrived at Bess's house, Bess's mother was in the front yard raking leaves.

George had come alone because Will was watching a football game with her dad.

"Bess is in her room," Mrs. Marvin said, worry written all over her. "Go right up. And, George," she said, dropping her voice, "see if you can get through to her. She's so distant."

"I know," George commiserated. "I'll try."

Bess's door was open, and she was on the phone when George walked in. She waved with her good arm and mouthed, "I'll be off in a sec."

"No rush," George mouthed back, and shifted a stack of Bess's clothes to make room for herself on a chair.

A sappy love scene filled the screen of Bess's small TV, but the sound was off.

"I know, Brian, it's good to hear your voice, too," Bess said in a monotone.

Brian Daglian. George smiled at the thought of Bess's good friend and theater buddy.

"No, Brian, I haven't really thought much about my audition for Jeanne Glasseburg's class." Bess pressed her hand to her temple. "Hey, Bri—I've got to go now, okay?"

Brian said something, then Bess said goodbye and hung up.

"That was Brian," she told George, and picked up the remote. She punched the volume button.

George jumped up and planted herself in front of the television.

"Hey, what are you doing?" Bess cried.

"No, Bess. I'm not going to let you do this anymore." George reached over and turned the

TV off. "When people are around, you don't need to watch this stuff."

Bess looked as if she were about to muster up the energy to protest. She treated George to a halfhearted glare, then tossed the remote aside and shrugged. "Whatever."

George couldn't believe Bess gave up her TV so easily. She would have preferred more of an argument from her cousin. "Bess, we've got to talk."

"About what?"

"Come off it, Bess. Don't play games with me," George said. "You're not yourself."

Bess turned her back on George. "I don't know what you're talking about."

"Bess, you're shutting everyone out—your parents, Nancy, me."

George walked in front of Bess. She caught Bess's glance and held it. The circles under Bess's eyes seemed even bigger and darker than they had on Friday.

"I'm sorry, George." Bess's voice was barely a whisper, but it suddenly swelled with feeling. "I—I just feel—as if—" She struggled visibly to find the words. "As if someone took every nerve and bit of feeling out of my body. I want to cry for Paul, and I can't. George—I'm afraid." Bess got up and walked over to the window.

George watched her as Bess stared out the window. Bess didn't turn around, but she finally continued.

"Paul's never coming back. I don't know how

to live with that. I don't know how to cope with anything right now."

"Oh, Bess," George cried. "You're doing the best you can. But you can't hide in your room forever. You've got to start getting on with your life."

"Without Paul?" Bess asked.

"Nothing can change that now, Bess," George said, trying to put the picture of Paul out of her own head. "You should come back to school. Be with people, do the stuff you've always loved. You've still got all your friends, Bess."

"I know." Bess sighed. She sank down onto the bed, and George sat next to her. "I'm not sure I want to go back to Wilder. Everything there will remind me of him. At least he never was here.

"Maybe," she went on. "I should put my life on rewind. Start over again, someplace new, fresh." A weak smile crossed her lips. "I was thinking of writing some letters to a couple of the other schools that I got into to see if I can start up someplace else in spring semester."

George swallowed hard. Life at Wilder without Bess? George couldn't begin to picture that.

"My parents," Bess confided grudgingly, "think I shouldn't be deciding anything now. They say I need to talk to some kind of counselor." Bess took George's hand. "I don't want to do that. I want to handle this on my own. I don't need a counselor. Do I?"

Bess looked so upset that George tried to

phrase her answer carefully. "Bess, remember when your roommate, Leslie, was in trouble? You told her to see a counselor."

"Leslie? I'm not like her," Bess protested. "She was a mess. I'm not a mess—not like that."

"No, you're not," George said to soothe her quickly. "But you've been through something awful. Counselors are there to help you deal with crises in your life."

Bess stared at George, then burst into tears. George gathered her in her arms and felt tears start down her own face. Bess sobbed and sobbed, until George was sure she had no more tears.

"Bess, it's okay. It's good to cry."

"I'm not crazy. I don't want to see a counselor," Bess wailed into George's shoulder.

"Don't think about that now," George said. "Just cry it out. You'll feel better. You don't have to see a counselor or anything if you don't want to. You don't even have to go back to Wilder." She only wished she could find a way to get Bess to focus on how much Leslie had been helped by a bit of counseling.

Slowly Bess's tears subsided. "Do you think I have to see a counselor right now?"

George shook her head. "Not if you don't want to. You have to do what you think is right for you. One step at a time."

"Thanks," Bess said, blowing her nose. "It did help to talk, really."

"Yeah. Well, it's not good just to hold everything in," George told her. George managed to sound calm and confident, but inside she was reeling. Until then she'd never stopped to think what life might be like for her without Bess at Wilder.

The town of Keelor Falls was decked out for the festival. Banners were strung between the old brick storefronts that lined the Victorian village's main street. Nancy had always loved the historic small town. As long as she could remember, Keelor Falls had been known for its beautiful shops, handmade clothing, and galleries, but mostly for its twice-a-year festivals.

Merchants were running sidewalk sales, and the town park was full of out-of-town vendors selling their wares. As Nancy strolled through the open-air aisles of display tables, a lively bluegrass trio played in the bandshell. The upbeat music matched her mood perfectly.

She was having a good time. And not in spite of Avery but because of her. Nancy couldn't believe it, but she was almost okay with Avery today, not quite like she'd been back at Wilder the weekend she'd first met her, but close to it.

Avery obviously felt the same way. Nancy noticed her quiet eyes were shining as she stopped in front of a display of handwoven chenille sweaters. As Avery went behind a curtain to try on a sweater, Jake took Nancy's elbow.

"See, life with Avery isn't all that bad," he

pointed out. "I told you if you give it time, you two will hit it off just fine."

Nancy's mood darkened slightly. "Jake, you're right. I am having a good time," she whispered, making sure Avery couldn't overhear them, "but don't be smug about it."

"You just don't want to admit you were wrong," Jake teased.

Nancy gritted her teeth. "This has nothing to do with right and wrong." She wanted to explain how she'd been feeling, but when she saw Jake's face, she gave up. Jake had only been trying to make her feel better, but he didn't seem to understand that her issues with Avery weren't all black and white.

She let out a frustrated sigh, then said, "Oh, why bother? You just don't get it."

With that, Nancy marched to the next table. It featured ceramic jewelry. Seeing earrings on the table, she remembered Jeff and Kate. She hadn't bothered to track them down yet. When Avery, Jake, and her dad strolled up, she suggested they split up awhile and meet a little later to have their picnic lunch.

"Jake and I have some friends here from Wilder," she told Avery. "We want to find out if they know anything about the duffel bag mix-up and the tapes."

So while Carson Drew and Avery went off to a gallery, Nancy and Jake searched for Kate and Jeff. They had canvassed half the exhibits before Nancy spotted Jeff. "Kate's not with him," she said as they approached the table. The display was almost identical to the one she'd seen outside the Student Union. Earrings on one end of the table, tapes on the other.

"Look at those earrings," Jake murmured.

Nancy already had. They were similar to the earrings Kate had been wearing back at Wilder—and the one Nancy had found outside the kitchen door the night before.

"Hi, Jeff," Nancy said breezily, fingering the earrings. Meanwhile Jake was casually flipping through the tapes. Good! Nancy thought.

Jeff looked at her a moment, as if trying to place her. "Oh, hi," he said.

"This is Jake Collins," Nancy said, and Jake reached out to shake Jeff's hand.

Jeff held back a second. "Jake Collins?" he repeated, a hint of a question in his voice. Nancy watched him take a good look at Jake before finally smiling. "Glad to meet you," he said. He paused and asked casually, "You go to Wilder, too?"

Jake nodded.

"George and her friend Will said they ran into you yesterday, up at the falls," Jake said easily, still checking out the tapes.

"Uh—right. Kate's friends." This time Nancy noticed that Jeff swallowed hard.

He reached under the table and grabbed a bag. "Sorry, but you came at a bad time. I'm sort of trying to close up shop for lunch. Kate's not here," he said, speaking quickly. Right under

Nancy's nose, he began sweeping the tapes into a carryall bag.

"Oh, we were thinking of buying some tapes for the car," Jake said.

"Come back after lunch, then. I'll be here." Jeff bent down and zipped up the bag. Nancy and Jake exchanged a quick glance.

Jeff threw a cloth over the earring display and tucked his cashbox under his arm.

"Which way are you walking?" Jake asked, shoving his hands in his pockets. "Lunch sounds good."

"Oh." Jeff's expression became more nervous. "Probably the food tent."

"We'll walk with you," Nancy chimed in. "At least until something else grabs me. I love shopping," she said, smiling.

"Speaking of shopping, did you hear the other night on TV about the scam going on with counterfeit tapes?" Jake asked Jeff.

Jeff shook his head.

Nancy smiled to herself. She liked where Jake was taking this. "You might be interested," she said earnestly. "Since you're in the tape business and all. The market's being flooded with counterfeit tapes of some albums from famous groups, like the Cybersounds."

"That's bad," Jeff said, sounding calm.

Nancy plunged on. "The news show I saw had some woman from the Justice Department saying that whoever's masterminding the scheme would be looking at some pretty heavy prison time."

"In federal prison," Jake said. "Since they've been selling tapes across state lines."

Nancy scrutinized Jeff. He still looked nervous, but he managed a shrug. "Look, I don't really care since I'm not selling anything illegal."

Nancy saw Jeff's expression shift from nervousness to real worry. He was staring over her shoulder and looked as if he'd just seen a ghost.

Nancy followed his gaze. She glimpsed the back of a bright red jacket. The girl wearing it was vaguely familiar, but the crowd swallowed her up before Nancy saw her face.

"I'm stuffed!" Ginny pretended to stagger down the path outside Java Joe's as she clutched her stomach.

Frank Chung laughed. He poked his finger against Ginny's sleeve. "You don't look stuffed. You still look pretty slim to me."

Ginny cracked up and thought how great it felt to laugh and talk and just feel normal again. She couldn't remember how long it had been since she'd felt more like herself.

Wrong, Ginny countered in the next breath. She knew exactly how long it had been. She could count the days and nights since she'd broken up with Ray.

She suddenly felt wistful. Frank was nice, but he wasn't Ray. Frank must have sensed her change of mood.

"Hey, what's up?"

Ginny shrugged. "Nothing." She grinned at

Frank, and her blues floated away like a cloud in a breeze.

"Do you work at the hospital today or tomorrow?" Frank asked as they headed for Thayer Hall.

"No. I was just booked for yesterday."

"You sound sad about having a couple of days off," Frank remarked.

"Weird, isn't it?"

"Not really." Frank was definite. "When I'm painting in the studio I can never get enough of it."

Ginny stopped and looked at Frank. The bare trees were reflected in his glasses, and he looked serious and earnest. This was a guy, she decided, who felt comfortable with himself and his decisions. "You really mean that?"

"I do. Why?"

"Oh, I don't know," Ginny said, but she did know. She didn't feel on the defensive about what she longed for in her life. It was good to follow her heart, even if it led her into practicing medicine and not writing song lyrics.

"So here we are. Back where we started." Frank's voice broke into Ginny's thoughts. She looked up. They were in front of her dorm. Maybe she'd invite Frank into the lounge, to talk some more. Then she spotted a familiar old car.

Her easy mood went up in smoke.

"Ray?" she said.

Frank followed her gaze.

Ray was rolling down the window of the car. He looked terrible.

Ginny's heart stopped. Wasn't he supposed to be in Chicago?

"Ray?" she cried, and started for the car.

"Ginny?"

At the sight of her, his mouth lifted into a smile. Then he spotted Frank behind her, and his face changed. She had never seen anyone look so hurt.

When she reached the car, he was already turning the key in the ignition.

"Ray, what are you doing here?" she asked. "Frank and I just went to brunch, and . . ."

"Look, I've got to go," he mumbled, not glancing at her. He gunned the engine, then pulled away, the gravel crunching under his wheels.

"What's with Ray?" Frank asked.

"I don't know," Ginny said, barely able to find her voice. "But whatever it is, it's bad."

CHAPTER 11

Jake," Nancy said, gripping his arm and directing his attention away from Jeff. "See that girl in the red jacket? The one with the short dark hair? I know her from somewhere."

Jake craned his neck and looked past the open flap of the festival food tent. He spotted the girl, small and slight, quickly weaving her way through the crowd. "She doesn't look familiar to me," he said.

"I can't place her, but I've seen her before," Nancy said. "Hey! Where's Jeff?"

Jake glanced around the food tent. Jeff had vanished. "Split," he replied. "He sure wasn't in the mood to talk to us."

"You can say that again," Nancy remarked, following Jake onto the fairway.

Jake shielded his eyes from the sun, but Jeff

was nowhere in sight. "Didn't you get the feeling that as soon as you introduced me by name, he got just a little uptight?"

Nancy smiled grimly. "Just a little." She frowned and added, "That's when he tried to hide those tapes from you, too. And just now, did you see his face when he spotted that girl?"

"Is that what happened?" Jake replied, remembering clearly how Jeff had paled. "How does he know her?"

"From Wilder, probably. That's where *I* think I know her from," Nancy said. A second later she exclaimed, "Now I remember! She was in my dorm room, looking for that red jacket she was wearing today. Kara had borrowed it from her and forgot to give it back. Her name is . . ." Nancy closed her eyes to think.

Nancy's face lit up. "Lily. That's her name. I remember now. Let's try to find her," she said. "I'm sure Jeff knows her. The sight of her really freaked him out."

"Let's get back to his booth," Jake urged.

But the crowd had thickened, and their progress down the fairway was maddeningly slow. Halfway there, Nancy spotted Kate Terrell. She seemed very worried. "Oh, Nancy," she said, "I'm really freaked."

"What happened? We saw Jeff at his table."

"I know," Kate replied. "He told me just now when I got back from lunch. But Jeff has gone completely weird on me." She took a breath. "Okay, I'm not making sense. Come here." She motioned Nancy and Jake over to a spot out of the crowd. "Yesterday we ran into George and Will hiking up at the falls."

"George mentioned that," Nancy said.

Kate went on. "George mentioned a mix-up with Jake's bag and some tapes. Jeff got really nervous at the mention of those tapes. I asked him what was wrong, but he wouldn't talk about it."

"So?" Jake urged her to go on.

"Just after he spoke to both of you at the table, he really lost it. When I got back he was packing up everything. He said we're leaving now. But it's early. He's been doing good business, too." Kate was obviously confused. "What's going on?"

Jake and Nancy exchanged a glance. Jake nodded. "Some of the tapes Jeff is selling might be counterfeit," Nancy told her. Kate looked stunned.

"Jeff wouldn't do that. I know he wouldn't," Kate said.

"Maybe. Maybe not," Jake said. "But ever since that mix-up with my duffel bag, weird things have been happening. Nancy's car was broken into either Friday night or Saturday. And there was another break-in at her house on Saturday night."

"But why?" Kate asked. "What's this got to do with Jeff?"

"Some of the counterfeit tapes were in my car and in the house," Nancy said. "Whoever owns the tapes wanted to get them and probably wanted to sell them at the festival. In any event they didn't plan on having their illegal stuff fall into our hands."

"Well, I can tell you one thing for sure, Nancy. Jeff didn't break into your house *or* car. Friday night we didn't leave Wilder until really late. And Saturday morning we had a long breakfast before we went hiking and ran into George. Then last night we were together all night."

Something about the way Kate told her story made Jake believe her. Still, Jake thought, Kate might be shielding Jeff. They were dating.

"Kate," Nancy asked, "do you know someone named Lily? She goes to Wilder."

"Lily?" Kate looked startled. "Sure. Lily Capeci. She makes all the earrings Jeff sells."

Jake cleared his throat. "Known her long?"

"No, not really." Kate gave a slight laugh. "Actually, I've never met her, just talked to her on the phone. She's Jeff's friend, kind of a business partner, really. She's never been around when I'm with him. He likes to keep his business stuff separate from personal things. I'm just helping out here, so I could see him this weekend."

"How'd Jeff get involved in selling earrings and tapes at these fairs?" Jake asked, keeping one eye on the shoppers traveling the fairway. He was hoping to spot Lily's red jacket.

"Lily used to sell the earrings herself at the fairs," Kate replied. "Jeff told me she became friends with some people she met at the crafts fairs who sold cassettes. They said it was really easy to sell them, and Lily wanted to try, so her friends set her up with the distributors of the cassettes. But with the tapes and earrings, she ended up with more business than she could handle and still go to school. She and Jeff were friends, and she asked if he'd like to take over part of her business."

"I imagine you can make a lot of money at one of these fairs," Jake said.

"Sure. Jeff says just working weekends in the spring and fall seasons you can make practically your whole tuition for a semester. Anyway, Lily got Jeff involved and set him up. That's about it."

She stopped and looked intently at Jake and Nancy. "Hey, why did you ask about Lily?"

"I just saw her—and so did Jeff, I think."

"She's here?" Kate looked surprised. "But why? She gave Jeff her new supply of earrings before we left Wilder. Jeff met her in Weston and picked them up."

"You didn't go with him?" Jake asked.

Kate shrugged. "No. I had errands to run."

"Thanks a lot, Kate, for telling us all this," Nancy said.

"Yeah, well, I want you to know Jeff isn't a dishonest person."

"I'd like to believe that," Nancy said, sounding as if she really meant it.

Kate left to look for Jeff, while Jake and Nancy made their way to the picnic area.

Avery was waving at them from a table, and

Jake waved back. "What should we do about Jeff and Kate?"

Nancy shook her head. "Beats me. We can't *prove* anything, and besides, they're leaving now."

"So then we're free for the rest of the day?" Jake asked.

"For what?" Her eyes were laughing.

"For fun, and for enjoying what's left of our double date with your dad and"—he hesitated ever so slightly—"Avery." All weekend long he never knew what kind of reaction Avery's name might provoke in Nancy.

To his relief Nancy's expression didn't change. "I'm ready for fun," she said easily. "We can worry about Kate and Jeff when we get back to Wilder."

"Not even the most driven, dedicated radio fan could find us here," Tim said to Kara as they sat on the grass beside Wilder's small lake.

The frigid wind made Kara clutch the striped stadium blanket tighter around her chest, and she wished she was wearing long underwear beneath her jeans. She laughed at Tim through chattering teeth. "Such a person *could* find us here, but why risk frostbite looking for us? What two people in their right minds would be having lunch by the lake on such a cold day?"

Tim got up and turned the hot dogs on the grill, then settled back down with his head in Kara's lap. "We are not in our right minds. We are definitely, totally nuts, and we like it that way." Tim flashed a boyish, adoring smile in Kara's face.

She bent low to kiss him. "You're a real find, Tim Downing. Not many guys would indulge me like this, with a surprise picnic by the lake."

"*I* indulge *you?* I'm the one who wanted to hide from the world for the afternoon. Every time you open your mouth, someone recognizes your voice. Now only I can hear you."

Kara batted him with the fringe of her blanket. "Not true," she contradicted. "*Everyone* on campus doesn't recognize my voice—not yet." But Kara loved it when they did.

"Kara?"

She turned around. One of her Pi Phi sisters was jogging down the path that circled the lake. Kara frantically tried to remember her name. "Amy?" she tried.

"Alison!" the girl corrected with a smile. She didn't look very upset. She ran in place as she talked. "You and Montana and Nikki did a really cool job on the radio show."

Kara glowed. "Thanks," she said, trying to sound modest. But secretly—no, not even secretly—she loved the praise. "Glad you liked it."

"I did," Alison said. "But you should ask Patrice what she thinks."

"Why?" Kara asked, and looked up at Alison. "She didn't even hear it."

"She heard a tape of it. And some of her friends called and told her *all* about it."

Kara's heart swelled with pride.

"Does she seem ticked off!" Allison announced.

"What?" Tim and Kara said in unison.

"Yeah, about how you guys changed the topic and were so unprofessional about the commercials and all that tech stuff. She's ready to kill."

"Oh no!" Kara said.

"I'd make myself scarce for a while until she calms down. Patrice is due back tomorrow."

Kara sat in stunned silence. For the first time, words failed her.

"Since this is the last breakfast I'm cooking for you for a while," Hannah said on Monday morning, "I've made it extra special." The housekeeper bustled in from the kitchen bearing a tray full of homemade biscuits and sausage.

"It smells incredible," Jake said, rubbing his hands together.

Nancy eyed the heavy breakfast skeptically. "Hannah, you don't have to do all this, you know. Cereal and fruit would have been okay."

"There's nothing special about that," Hannah huffed.

"Why do we have to act like this is such a big special occasion? I came home for the weekend, that's all." The more Nancy thought about all this fuss, the more annoyed she became. "It's not like I'm a guest here or anything."

"But Jake is," Carson Drew reminded her, looking up from his paper.

"Don't listen to Nancy," Jake said, touching her hand. "She's afraid you're all spoiling me."

Nancy yanked her hand away from Jake's. "I don't need spoiling in my own house. If you need to spoil someone around here, try Avery." She clamped her mouth shut.

Hannah's face fell at Nancy's comment. Carson Drew folded his paper with a snap. "Nancy, that remark about Avery was uncalled for."

"Carson," Avery said. "I'm sure Nancy didn't mean—"

"How do you know what I meant?" Nancy broke in, her voice rising. "You don't know the first thing about me, Avery. You don't know how I feel about what's going on in this house. I hate how I'm being treated this weekend."

"I'd say you've been treated very well." Her father sounded angry.

"Right—as if I were a stranger here. Dad, this is my house, too. I don't need to be catered to like some kind of guest."

"Nancy," Hannah said, "no one thinks you're a guest here."

"Then stop acting like I am."

"Nancy," her dad said, his voice high, "I don't know what's wrong, but you have no reason to talk to Hannah like that. And what did you mean, 'what's going on in this house'?"

Nancy glared back at her father. "All the changes. I hate them. I don't see why the minute I leave for college you have to start tearing the place apart."

"Nancy," Avery broke in, "nothing's been torn apart."

"You're changing everything, Avery. The furniture, the colors of the walls. Next time I come home it's not going to feel like home. And you'd better not touch my room."

"Nancy, stop this!" Carson Drew said. "I can't believe you're acting this way. I'd say you owe both Hannah and Avery an apology."

Nancy pursed her lips. Apologize? Never. How dare he embarrass her in front of everyone! She glared back at her father, a tightness constricting the back of her throat. Great, she realized, now I'm going to cry.

She balled up her napkin and was about to bolt to her room when the phone rang. Nancy was nearest, and she grabbed it before the second ring, silently blessing the god or goddess of good timing. "Hello?"

She swallowed hard.

"Is Jake Collins there? Nancy, is that you?"

"Nick? Yeah, hi. Just a minute, Jake's right here." Nancy looked back over her shoulder at Jake, who got up and took the phone.

Nancy started out of the room. "Nancy," Jake called after her. "Why don't you listen in?"

Nancy went into the den and closed the door. She took a deep breath and tried to still her pulse. What had just happened out there at the table? She had never had such a fight with her father in her whole life. And having him talk to her as if she were a child, in front of everyone—

146

how humiliating! She was so mad at him, she couldn't think straight.

Closing her eyes a moment, pausing to collect herself, Nancy pictured her father's shocked and angry face. Then she saw something else—his expression was one of deep hurt, too. Guilt washed over her. And Hannah . . . how could she insult Hannah like that? Nancy opened her eyes. "I wish Avery had never walked into our lives," she said out loud.

"Nancy?" Jake called from the hall. "Have you picked up yet?"

Nancy picked up the receiver of the phone on the desk. "Hi, I'm here." Her throat still ached from wanting to cry.

"So, Nick, what's up? Nancy knows about the tapes."

"I spoke to Ed," Nick said. "He told me the whole story. When he began stocking Ed's Music World he was using a lot of distributors. Most he knew from his other downtown store, but some guys were new to him. One of the new sales reps offered him a great deal on the Cybersounds tapes. Ed had no idea they were counterfeit, not until one of his other distributors clued him in. By then the tapes had been on the shelves for a day already."

"So that's when that kid bought them," Nancy commented on her end of the phone.

"Right." Nick continued, "Ed took the tapes off the shelves and put the box in my car to bring home until he could contact the distributing company about what to do with the tapes. He also wanted to find out how the rep got the counterfeits originally. Ed wanted to store the tapes away from the business so no one would get them mixed up with the other stock, and put them on the shelves again. He doesn't want this to mess up his business."

"So that's why he pretended never to have had the tapes to begin with," Nancy surmised.

"Yes. It threw him. Anyway, we just got a call this morning from the distributor. Turns out that one particular sales rep had decided to make money on the side by dealing in counterfeit and bootlegged material, along with his legit stuff. He was fired and arrested earlier today."

"Great!" Jake said. "I knew you and Ed weren't in on anything illegal."

"But things must have looked a little sticky there for a while. I understand, Jake. Look, I've got to go. I'm putting in a few more hours at my uncle's store. See you back at the apartment tonight."

Nancy hung up the phone and thought for a moment. She was glad that Nick and his uncle were in the clear. Her eye fell on the duffel bag stuffed under her father's desk. Whom did it belong to? Nancy felt certain that Lily was deep in the counterfeit scheme and probably involved in burgling her car as well as the house.

The earring Nancy had found was certainly a clue. Lily probably wore the earrings she made. Nancy only had to connect Lily to the duffel.

She looked through the bag. All the tapes were still there, with the bundled-up T-shirts. Nancy's hand closed on something metal. The key! Of course, the key to a locker in the Weston bus station.

Nancy jumped up. She had a strong hunch the proof of Lily's connection to the tapes and the counterfeiters would be in that locker.

"Jake?" she called, going out into the hall to find him. He was heading in her direction.

"Good news? About Nick, I mean."

"Terrific news. But, Jake, we have to get going."

"What's the rush?"

Nancy noticed he was staring back toward the dining room. Avery and Nancy's father were still at the table. Nancy's stomach knotted up again.

"I've got an idea about Lily. Let's get back to Weston early and check out the bus station."

"Why?"

Nancy waved the locker key in Jake's face. "I think that whatever is in that locker will incriminate Lily. I'm more sure than ever she's the missing link in this counterfeiting scheme. And I want to find out who broke into my house and car. That's really made me mad."

"Okay. I can be ready to go in ten minutes."

Nancy pocketed the key, then backtracked to the study and picked up the duffel.

Jake followed her. "Are you going to try to smooth things out before you leave?" Jake gestured toward the dining room. Nancy detected a critical note in his voice.

"No, I can't deal with them now," she responded tightly. "I'm just going to tell my dad about our change of plans." She started for the dining room. Jake pulled her aside.

"Nancy," he said. Though he spoke in an undertone, Nancy could hear he was annoyed. "Look, Avery and your dad have their life, and you've got yours. Your father's found a woman to make him happy, and maybe to share his home. That's his business. I can't believe you're not happy for him. But that's your problem, not Avery's. You should apologize before you go."

Nancy pulled her arm away and glared at him. "Jake, you obviously haven't a clue what I'm feeling. So just stay out of it. I'll smooth things out in my own good time."

Nancy had no idea how. She only knew that her life had changed enough in the past few months, and this house wasn't her only home anymore. She had another life at Wilder, and the time had come to move ahead, away from River Heights, away from her dad and Hannah. She worked up her nerve and walked into the dining room.

Avery looked up, her expression guarded. Her father kept reading the paper. Nancy's stomach churned.

"Dad, something's come up, and Jake and I have to get back to school."

Carson Drew put his paper down and eyed

Nancy carefully. "We need to sit down and talk," he suggested quietly.

"I know," Nancy agreed, just wanting to get out of there. "But I can't now. We've got to go."

Her father's face registered anger, hurt, and disappointment. "All right. Call if you need to talk—about anything."

"I will, Dad," Nancy said. "I promise."

It wasn't until she got in the car a little later that she realized she hadn't said goodbye to Avery or Hannah or hugged her dad.

CHAPTER 12

Stephanie?" Ginny said in surprise early Monday morning. "What are you doing up? There are no classes today."

"I'm working an extra shift at the old sweatshop," Stephanie answered. "Oh, and good morning to you, too," she called back over her shoulder as Ginny disappeared into the bathroom.

Stephanie had planned her outfit carefully for that day. She'd be wearing slim black pants and a rusty red sweater that set off her tan and her long black hair. Since there were no classes until Tuesday, she had taken on another shift at Berrigan's. She could use the money, thanks to her father canceling her credit cards.

Thinking about her dad reminded Stephanie of their phone conversation the other day, and his dumb remark about love and him and Kiki.

The other reason she'd planned to work every day that weekend at Berrigan's had been Jonathan. She wanted to spend as much time with him as possible.

Or part of her did. Another part of her wanted to cool it, to keep him at arm's length. He had a way of getting under her skin, into her head. But she couldn't stop thinking about him, remembering not just the way he touched her but the way he shared his thoughts with her. The way he tried to draw her out. She kept holding back, but she felt as if she was fighting a losing battle.

She had managed Saturday night to keep the talking to a minimum, and he hadn't minded. She wanted to date him, but Stephanie wasn't sure she was ready for anything more serious.

Except, she told herself, just one day without him and she felt as if she was going through some sort of withdrawal. Right now she couldn't wait until she saw him.

She felt energized as she started off for Berrigan's. It wasn't until she arrived at the employees' entrance to the downtown department store that she realized she hadn't even had a second morning cigarette.

She walked into the employee locker room humming under her breath. Stephanie opened her locker and spotted an envelope on the bottom of it. Someone must have slipped it through a vent in the door.

She picked it up and turned it over. Nothing was written on the outside. When she opened it, something fell out onto the floor and rolled just under her locker. She bent and retrieved it. "Oh!" she gasped. It was a small ring in the form of two tiny hands clasped together. Inside the envelope was a card. Stephanie read the message: "Here's to being more than just friends— Jonathan."

Stephanie put her hand to her mouth. A warm feeling spread from the middle of her chest all the way out to her fingertips. She had the craziest urge to hug someone.

This guy *really* likes me, she thought, slamming her locker shut. The ring proved it.

Stephanie slipped the ring on her finger and held her hand out to stare at it. It wasn't very expensive, and not at all the kind of thing she imagined wearing. But it was perfect.

With a big smile on her face, she went out to the sales floor. Jonathan really likes me. The words had scarcely run through her mind when she saw him, his back toward her.

Jonathan was standing by the door, talking to one of the security guards. Stephanie stopped in the middle of the aisle, entranced by the sight of him. She wanted to walk up and say thank you. But she was afraid. She looked down at the ring. What did it mean, exactly? How serious were things getting? Her throat tightened. She turned her back on Jonathan and started for the cosmetics counter.

"Stephanie?" His voice pierced her.

She hesitated before facing him. She looked

down and saw the ring on her finger. "Jonathan," she said, turning around. "Thank you. I love it." She couldn't keep the smile off her face.

"Good, because I meant it," he said, touching the ring. His smile matched hers, and they just stared at each other.

Jonathan cleared his throat. Stephanie noticed the color rise to his cheeks. People were watching them.

"Thanks," Stephanie said. "I'm glad." She turned her back on him and floated to the cosmetics counter.

As she counted the change in her register, she suddenly realized that whatever was happening with Jonathan, it was too late to stop it, even if she wanted to.

Bess watched from her living-room window until the taillights of Nancy's car disappeared around the corner. It had been sweet of Nancy, Jake, George, and Will to drop by on their way back to Wilder.

Still, a part of Bess was glad to see them go. They'd all been treating her as if she was sick. Everyone was worried about her, and Bess didn't like it.

But now that they were gone, she felt more alone than ever. Her parents were at work, and she roamed from room to room, not sure what to do with herself. She finally beat a trail back to the TV and the programs that numbed her and kept her from thinking too much—about Paul, about Wilder.

Wilder? Bess's attention wandered from the TV show. She felt funny—a little left out—not driving back to school with her friends.

She tried to focus on the TV again, but instead she kept thinking about the weekend. It *had* felt good to talk and cry with George. George had mentioned counseling, just as her parents had.

Bess gnawed her lip. She wasn't sure she could face that. She didn't want to talk about Paul, especially to a stranger. Still, George thought counseling would help her get back on track with school, and the rest of her life.

Bess couldn't begin to picture the rest of her life. However it turned out, she was sure her life would be easier if she never thought about Paul again. But *that* was impossible. Especially if she went back to Wilder.

While Bess sat thinking, the doorbell suddenly rang. She padded to the front hall and opened the door.

"Ned!"

"I wanted to say goodbye before I headed back to school," Ned said. "Can I come in?"

"Oh." Bess stood back and held the door open more. "Sure, I wasn't thinking."

She ushered Ned into the living room and turned off the TV. She stood there looking up at all six feet of him. Good old solid Ned. Bess found herself smiling.

Ned smiled back. "Now, that's better," he said, and brushed her cheek with his finger.

The gesture startled Bess. It reminded her of her last day with Paul. He had done something just like that before they got on that crazy motorcycle. Bess's whole chest heaved, and she thought she was about to explode. A heartbeat later she broke down into sobs.

"Bess?"

"I'm sorry," she cried, and a second later she was in Ned's arms. He led her to the sofa. Bess felt him stroke her head as she sobbed into his chest. It felt good to be held.

After what seemed like hours, Bess realized her sobs had quieted. Finally she was able to sit up. She felt awkward and silly for breaking down. "I'm sorry." She gulped. Ned grabbed some tissues from the table and handed them to her. Bess mopped up her tears and blew her nose.

"I don't know what happened there—I suddenly remembered that last day with Paul."

Ned just sat there and held her hand. "What was Paul like?" he asked.

A torrent of emotions washed over Bess. She looked up, startled, and stared at Ned. He was smiling at her. "Tell me."

Bess began to smile back. What was Paul like? She could tell Ned about his wonderful golden looks: his hair, his beautiful eyes, the tan that seemed as if it would never fade. The laugh lines around his eyes. But *funny* was one of the things that came to mind. "He was funny," she said.

"Yeah?"

"Yeah." Bess bit her lip as she searched her memory for the perfect example to make Ned understand. "Not class-clown funny. Just a great sense of humor. And he was a really kind guy." Bess leaned back against the couch.

"When I got to Wilder I was one crazed person. I got involved in everything and anything. I met Paul right away, but I never had the time to go out with him. So he gave me a goofy date book. He'd penciled in ten-minute time periods when we could meet or have coffee—or whatever. He was determined that we'd spend time together." Bess savored the memory.

Then she told Ned about the bogus treasure hunt Paul set up for her, just to lure her to a private spot in the university greenhouse, where they shared their first kiss.

Ned laughed. "That's pretty creative."

Bess nodded and smiled. "Creative. Paul was that and smart, too. He was the kind of guy who could get people together and manage things." She tucked her legs under her and said enthusiastically, "He helped put together one of the best fund-raisers at Wilder—a casino event called Black and White Nights." She then launched into the story of the fund-raiser.

Once she started, she couldn't stop talking about Paul. Suddenly the clock chimed three times. "Ned, you've been here for an hour!" She stood up. "I'm so sorry. You should have left for Emerson."

"Bess, it's okay," Ned said. "I've enjoyed hearing about Paul. I would have liked to have known him."

Bess studied her feet a moment. She looked up at Ned through a veil of tears. She actually smiled as she wiped them away. "Yes, you would have." Then she realized something. "You're right, you know. It was good talking about him."

"Talking helps. You also have Nancy and George to talk to, Bess. They love you, too."

"I know." Bess thought of how her two best friends had been such a support since the accident. "Ned?" she blurted out suddenly. "What do you think about counseling? My parents think I need to talk to a counselor."

Ned became serious. "That's not a bad idea. You should think about it, Bess. Counselors help lots of people. But it's your decision."

"Yes," said Bess, feeling the first stirrings of hope. First George, now Ned thought it was a good idea. "Yes, I'm thinking about it."

Bess suddenly felt hungry. "Hey, want some lunch?" she asked Ned.

"I'm starved," he admitted. "But I don't want to tire you out or anything."

"I'm cool," Bess said, leading him into the kitchen. "I'll need some help, though." She pointed to her broken arm.

Ned leaned back and eyed the cast critically. "Hey, no one's signed it yet."

Bess looked down at the dingy white surface. "No, no one has."

"Then let me do the honors," Ned said, selecting a felt-tip marker from a mug full of pens on the counter. He scribbled "With love," then signed his name. They made sandwiches and talked more. Then Ned left.

Bess walked into the study and rummaged in her father's desk for some material about grief counseling that he'd tried to give her earlier. She found the folder and sat down to read it.

Monday's soap opera episodes were over for hours before Bess thought to turn on the TV.

"Ah, for a greasy burger at the Bumblebee Diner," Jake remarked as they passed the Weston eatery on their way to the bus depot.

"What?" George mocked from the backseat of Nancy's car. "Didn't you like Hannah's cooking?"

Jake glanced quickly at Nancy. "Speaking for myself, Hannah's cooking was great."

"What did I say?" George asked Nancy.

"I don't want to talk about it." Nancy tried to keep her tone light, but her heart was heavy. Her weekend had not turned out as she'd hoped it would. Jake hadn't been the problem, she had.

Thinking of how she'd behaved made her ashamed, but she was still angry about Avery's being in her house and about the way her father had spoken to her. And no one—except Ned—seemed to understand. Nancy's home wasn't her home anymore, and she hated that. She really did.

"I hope you're right about Lily and the bus station locker," Will remarked. "I wouldn't have wanted to cut the weekend short for nothing."

"Yeah, I sure wasn't ready to come back," George said a little testily.

"Don't worry. I'm sure Nancy's on the right track," Jake said. He touched Nancy's hand, and she relaxed a little. Jake might not understand her, but he was still a pretty amazing guy. He never ceased to surprise her. He thought she was wrong for not apologizing to Avery, Hannah, and her father, but he dropped the whole thing once they got into the car.

He sensed she needed space, so he gave it to her. She took his hand and sighed. "I hope I'm right, too. I'd like to discover who's involved with those tapes and find out who broke into our house." She thought that would at least be something she could do for her dad.

"I just wish we could have spent more time with Bess," George said. "I think I was beginning to get through to her."

Nancy felt a pang of guilt. "I'm sorry, George."

"It's not your fault," George hurried to assure her. "Getting back early isn't so terrible in any case. But I'm hoping that Bess gets her act together enough to see a counselor."

"Her parents suggested that?" Jake asked.

"Yes," George said.

"But she's pretty reluctant," Will added.

"I hope she comes back to Wilder," Nancy

said. "I'll really miss her if she decides to change schools."

A few minutes later Nancy parked in front of the bus station. She fished in her pocket for the locker key. "The locker number's on the key," she told George and Will as they followed her and Jake into the depot. It took just a minute to find the locker.

"It's open!" Jake gasped.

Nancy cursed once under her breath. "I don't believe this."

"Lily got here before we did," Will said.

"Lily—or someone else," George suggested. "Maybe the person is still around."

Nancy checked out the small depot. Only a couple of people were in sight. Two men were in line in front of the ticket window, and the waiting area was deserted.

Finally Nancy spotted a maintenance man mopping the floor in front of another stand of lockers across the way.

"Excuse me," she said, walking up. "But why is this locker open?" She held up the key. "I have the key, and I didn't unlock it."

The man shoved his cap back. "Well"—he leaned on his mop—"when the time runs out—there's a two-week limit on the lockers—management opens them and stores any of the stuff for a while. In case someone comes to claim it."

He peered over his glasses at Nancy's key and read the number again. "But in this case a girl came in today, about fifteen minutes ago, and told the manager she'd lost her key. She described what was in the locker. When the manager opened it, the stuff was what she said, so it seemed that she was telling the truth." The man headed for a door marked Janitorial.

Nancy watched him, and her heart sank. "So we're too late."

They all stood in the waiting area a moment. "No point hanging around now," Jake finally said.

"Right," Nancy agreed.

"At least we know it was Lily," Will said, starting toward the entrance.

"He just said a girl," George reminded him. "Though ten-to-one it was Lily."

Nancy was only half-listening when a thought occurred to her. "The guy said she was just here, so I don't understand how we missed her." Nancy looked around the depot. The ticket counter took up one wall. Banks of lockers covered the other two. There was a janitor's closet, bathrooms, and a door marked Employees Only. But to the right of the bus boarding area was another door marked Exit.

"Maybe she took the back way out. She may not have gotten far," Nancy said.

"Come on," Jake said. "Let's look for her."

CHAPTER 13

Kara approached the side door of the library Monday morning and looked over her shoulder one more time. Good! No Patrice.

With any luck, Kara could continue to avoid her until she had a chance to see Montana and Nikki. She figured they had heard about Patrice's reaction to Saturday's show from the other Pi Phis. When she had dropped by the sorority house, Kara had been told that the girls had gone to the library to study.

Inside, Kara headed for the main reading room. Montana and Nikki were there at the center table. Montana spotted Kara and waved her over.

"Hi there," Montana said, a little too loudly. Heads turned.

"Come on!" Kara said, grabbing both girls and dragging them over to the stacks.

"What's with you?" Nikki said.

"Haven't you heard?" Kara whispered. "We're in trouble—big time!"

"Why?" Montana said.

"Patrice is looking to strangle us."

Nikki gaped in disbelief. "Strangle us? Why in the world . . ."

"Yes, why in the world!" a familiar voice repeated sarcastically.

Kara whirled around. "Patrice?" She gasped.

The tall, serious senior glared at them. "I trusted you guys. I put my own job at the radio station on the line, and look what you did!"

"What?" Nikki and Montana asked.

Kara just studied her sneakers.

"For one, Montana, you lied!"

"Never," Montana said.

"You said you knew how to run a radio show. Now KWDR can lose its license because of you airheads." Patrice began ticking off points on her fingers.

"Anyone listening to that show could tell that you girls had no idea what you were doing. You never gave the station ID. You forgot the commercials." Patrice paused, then continued.

"And you changed the topic without checking with me first."

Montana looked mortified. Nikki shrank back against the shelves. Kara felt awful. She had loved the show and being so popular.

There was a long silence, then Patrice cracked

the smallest smile. A second later she broke up laughing. "You should see your faces."

Kara raised her eyes from the floor.

"Your show was a big hit, even though you did mess everything up."

"So you liked it?" Kara asked.

Patrice gave a noncommittal shrug. "What I liked isn't the point." She was still smiling as she went on. "The station manager has been flooded with requests that you guys do a show again."

"What?" Montana, Nikki, and Kara chorused.

"Nutty—" Patrice said, looking positively gleeful. "But you guys have got yourself a show—almost."

"We do?" Kara shrieked, then clamped her hand over her mouth. Montana was grinning.

"I don't believe it!" Nikki whispered.

"The student station manager is trying to find you a time slot," Patrice said. "This could have been a disaster, but to tell you the truth, I'm happy. You guys can provide all the humor and light stuff, and I can do my thing—a more serious, issues-related show."

"So it all worked out great in the end," Kara said proudly.

"Yes," Patrice replied with a warning look. "But while you're here in the library, maybe you should look at a book on FCC rules and stuff."

Patrice left. As soon as she was out of sight, Nikki, Montana, and Kara hugged one another.

"People love us! We're hits!" Kara exclaimed, feeling like the luckiest person in the world.

*   *   *

Nancy headed back down the alley adjacent to the bus depot. She joined Jake and Will at the side door. George was already waiting for them.

"Lily wasn't in the bathroom," George said, catching her breath.

"I guess it was a long shot. Once she had her things, why should she stick around?" Nancy said, feeling dispirited as they filed back into the depot. Then she noticed the maintenance man was back, cleaning the outside of the lockers.

"Wait a minute," she said to her friends, and walked up to him.

"One more thing," she asked. "That girl, the one who claimed the stuff, was she small, about our age, with short dark hair?"

"And a red jacket?" Jake reminded.

The man nodded. "Sounds like her."

"So it could have been Lily," George said.

Nancy had another thought. "Did she have to do anything official to claim her stuff, once the manager opened the locker for her? Like sign a release, leave her name?"

"Sure. She went up to his office." He motioned vaguely to the door marked Employees Only.

Nancy didn't wait to hear the rest. "Let's go," she said, and raced across the waiting room, through the door, and up the steps.

"Why?" Will cried as they all followed her.

"She might still be there," Nancy yelled back.

"Nancy!" George called. "Down there!"

Nancy looked. At the end of the hall was a

room marked Office. Nancy ran to the door and pushed it open without bothering to knock.

A girl was bent over the desk, signing some papers. She had a carryall bag slung over her shoulder and a shoebox tucked under one arm. The man behind the desk looked up.

"Hey, what are you kids doing—"

The girl whirled around and gasped.

"Lily!" Nancy cried, not bothering to answer him. "Lost something?" She flourished the key in Lily's face.

At the sight of the key, Lily gripped the shoebox more tightly. She took a step toward the door as if she was going to leave. But Jake was blocking her only way out. Lily stared at them. "You're Kara's roommate, aren't you?" she asked Nancy. "What are you doing here?"

"Don't play dumb, Lily," Nancy said, feeling the anger rise in her. "I have a pretty good idea what you've been up to. Like breaking into my car over the weekend and trying to rob our house in River Heights. You scared my family half to death."

Lily scoffed. "You're nuts." Her big eyes met Nancy's boldly. Nancy noticed her earrings were exactly like the ones Jeff sold.

"Break-ins? Who got robbed?" The man behind the desk stood up. "What's going on here?"

"Don't listen to these people," Lily told the depot manager. "Besides, that guy stole my bag Friday night."

"Whatever gave you that idea?" Jake countered coolly. "You don't even know who I am."

Good thinking, Jake, Nancy thought as Lily paled slightly.

"But I can guess. If this is Nancy, you're Jake, her boyfriend. Kara's mentioned you," Lily said evenly, then pointed to the locker key Nancy still held in her hand. "If you didn't steal my bag, how'd you get my key?"

"You've got a lot of nerve!" George said.

Nancy intervened. "We found it. Jake picked up the wrong bag on Friday. There was no ID, but there were some counterfeit Cybersounds tapes."

"Counterfeit tapes?" The depot manager stepped out from behind his desk. He picked up the papers Lily had just signed and scanned them. When he looked up, his expression was serious.

"Let me see the contents of that box again," he said to Lily, reaching for the shoebox she was still holding.

"No way." She yanked the box away from him, but Nancy grabbed it. "That's mine!" Lily yelled, trying to get it back. The box tumbled to the floor, and a dozen or so shrink-wrapped Cybersounds tapes fell out, along with a small date book.

"Look!" Will cried. "There's the proof!" He bent down and hurriedly scooped up the tapes and the date book.

"These tapes are counterfeit?" the manager asked. "How do you know?"

"This album hasn't been released to stores yet," Nancy said.

The station manager frowned and picked up the phone. "I'm calling the police now. Whatever's going on, they'd better look into it."

"Don't!" Lily cried, flustered. "I don't know what these guys are talking about."

"We already know you're involved, Lily," Nancy said. "You and Jeff Rayburn."

"Jeff," Lily repeated. She pursed her lips and stared hard at Nancy. "Jeff told you?"

Nancy didn't answer. Jeff hadn't told anyone anything. But Lily's reactions confirmed Nancy's suspicions. Nancy held Lily's gaze and said, "Maybe you'd like to fill us in on the details until the police get here."

Lily narrowed her eyes and regarded Nancy. "You're bluffing."

"Am I?" Nancy said. "You're the one who just filled out forms claiming you lost the key to your locker, and this box full of Cybersounds tapes is yours. We found the key to the locker in the bag full of other bootlegged tapes."

Lily heaved a sigh. "Okay, so I am involved in selling tapes. I admit that. I had a new batch to give Jeff on Friday afternoon. But I didn't know they were counterfeits."

"Oh, come on, you don't expect anyone to believe that," Jake retorted.

Lily regarded him angrily. "You can't prove I knew the tapes were bootlegged."

"Maybe not," Nancy said. "But I'll bet there's

proof in this date book." She took the book from Will and started thumbing through it. "There are a lot of names and numbers in here. Could these be the distributors who supply you with tapes?"

Her words seemed to make an impression on Lily. Nancy noticed Lily's bravado evaporate a bit.

"And I'm sure the police will also find your fingerprints on my car and at my house," Nancy continued. "We have one of your earrings at my house. All of those things should prove breaking and entering."

Lily sighed and sat down heavily.

"The stupidest thing I did was leave that bag in the lobby at Thayer Hall," she said tersely. "When I realized I had the wrong one, I panicked. Not so much because of the tapes but because the key to the locker was inside. I had more tapes and my book in the locker.

"It's got the names and numbers of the contacts who supply me with tapes," Lily went on. "I couldn't risk you guys finding the key, checking the locker, and discovering this book."

"So you broke into my car and my house," Nancy stated, unable to keep the anger out of her voice.

"Yeah—well. It didn't work, did it?" She glared at Nancy.

Nancy glared back. "Go on," Jake said. "How did you know Nancy lived in River Heights?"

"I found your name and address in that duffel

bag you left at Thayer. It was easy to track you from that."

"But a guy called your apartment, Jake," George reminded him. "Not a girl."

Lily smirked. "I got a friend to call for me. Your roomie gave us Nancy's number. I checked and found out Keelor Falls wasn't far from River Heights.

"I drove down that night, found your house, and checked out your car. The bag wasn't there, though some of the tapes were. I figured you wouldn't know they were counterfeit, but to be on the safe side I took them anyway. Then I decided to go to Keelor Falls on Sunday to warn Jeff that we might be in trouble," Lily continued. "That someone had the bag and might be onto us. Besides, whoever found the bag could get into the locker, and my whole list of contacts would be lost."

"Jeff knew the tapes were counterfeit?" Will said sadly.

"He knew enough." Lily frowned. "When I got to Weston today I realized all at once that there had to be a way to get into the depot lockers without keys. People had to lose them all the time. Too bad I didn't think of it Friday night." Her dark eyes challenged Nancy, and her voice was insolent. "You never would have caught me."

The afternoon light slanted across Ray's bed. His guitar was propped up against the wall, all in shadows. It was still in its carrying case. He hadn't touched it since Chicago.

Ray sat in a corner on the floor, dejected. Just when he thought he had hit bottom, being fired from his own band, he'd made another stupid mistake.

He had believed—no, not believed, *trusted*— that Ginny would be there for him. Maybe they weren't dating anymore, but they'd just broken up. He hadn't thought she'd find someone so soon.

"Obviously I didn't mean as much to her as I thought," he growled to himself.

Just when he needed her, Ginny was off being perfectly happy with Frank Chung. Her *friend.* Even Ray wasn't stupid enough to believe that one.

Someone knocked on the door.

He walked heavily to the door and opened it.

"Ginny?" He couldn't believe his eyes. After the first surprise he realized she looked as if she'd been crying or something.

"Ray," she said, her voice trembling. "I ran into Spider about an hour ago in Weston." She pushed past Ray into his room. "I can't believe what's happened. He told me everything!"

It took Ray a second to find his voice. He walked back into the room, closing the door behind him. "Yeah—well. Then you know."

"I'm so sorry. This is really sick, Ray." Ginny leaned against the wall and folded her arms.

"How'd Spider seem about it?" Ray asked.

"Freaked, actually."

"But he hasn't changed his mind," Ray stated. He couldn't shake the feeling that maybe Spider had known about Pacific's plans all along.

"No, Ray," Ginny said quietly. "I mean, I didn't ask him, but he seemed to figure he was the new leader of the band." Ginny paused. "Ray, you can't be okay with this."

Ray gave a quick shake of his head. "No, of course not. I feel rotten. But it's my own fault, Ginny." He swallowed hard. "I shouldn't have trusted Roger. I didn't read the contract carefully enough. You know me: I always felt I didn't have to bother with stuff like that. Actually I wanted to tell you. You've been right all along."

"I have?"

"About not dropping out of school and needing to learn more. And about music not being enough."

"Ray," Ginny broke in. "Music is you. Period." She spoke with such passion that hope flickered in Ray's chest. Ginny cared that much.

"Right. I guess that's true," he said, wondering if he'd ever really feel like singing again.

"But it's sort of beside the point now." He shrugged and gazed out the window. "Joel Hoffman at Pacific Records gave me the impression that if I didn't give in about Spider taking over the lead, I might as well forget about ever signing with another label."

"He said that?" Ginny asked.

"Not outright," Ray admitted. "But he dropped some pretty big hints."

Ginny frowned. "Ray, that would be illegal. I think he was just trying to scare you."

"I don't know. These guys play hardball."

"True, but you're not a star yet. No point wasting time and money keeping you out of things."

Ray looked at her. "Gin, you're unbelievable. You're so practical sometimes."

Ginny cracked a small smile. "Not, as I remember, one of your favorite things about me."

"Don't," Ray said, but before he could go on, Ginny broke in.

"Ray, you're going to make music again. It might take a while, but you'll form another band, an even better one. The Beat Poets was step one for you. You're talented, Ray. You can't give up music. It's in your soul, Ray."

Ray couldn't take his eyes off Ginny. For a moment they just stared at each other, then Ginny quickly turned away.

He cleared his throat. "You're right. I have no choice but to make music. But meanwhile I'm going to major in business. I decided that if I had known more about contracts, I wouldn't have had to trust Spider's brother-in-law so much. I need to be more savvy about the business end of the recording industry." He smiled.

When he looked up, Ginny was smiling, too.

"Ray, that's great. I'm so proud of you."

"Ginny . . ." Ray took a step toward her, his whole being aching to hold her again. For a second he almost forgot about Frank Chung. But not quite. He stopped in his tracks and heaved a sigh. "So, how's Frank doing?"

"Fine," Ginny said, then frowned. "Ray, we just had brunch together."

"It's none of my business," Ray said quickly.

Ginny shook her head. "We're just friends. But"—she paused—"I guess it isn't your business, really."

They were silent a moment. Ray moistened his lips. "So, Ginny, did you work at the hospital this weekend?"

Ginny's eyes lit up. "Did I ever!" she said warmly. She looked as if she wanted to say more, but instead she got up. "Speaking of work. I'm due there in less than an hour."

Ray opened the door. They were very close, and Ray heard her catch her breath. Ginny slipped past him.

"I've got to go, Ray," she said in a quiet voice. "I still need—I need more time off."

"From us?"

"From us."

CHAPTER 14

Stephanie looked up from painting her nails a serious shade of red. It was late Monday night, and someone was struggling to open the door to her dorm room.

"Ah, the jet-setter returns." She greeted her roommate as Casey deposited shopping bags and her suitcase on the floor. Casey's short red hair looked disheveled, and her eyes were tired. "Casey, you look like you've had some major fun this weekend," Stephanie said with a smile.

Casey nodded and groaned. "I did, but it's over, and I'm beat." She flopped down on her bed with her coat on and smiled wanly at Stephanie. "Palm Springs was great, but now I need to rest." She struggled up to a sitting position and looked around the room. "Back to the old grind tomorrow."

"I take it that you and Charley had a good time," Stephanie remarked as Casey stood and began unpacking her clothes.

Casey smiled. "You could say that. And not much sleep."

Stephanie watched as Casey dreamily eyed the diamond ring on her left hand.

Stephanie touched her own ring. She hadn't taken Jonathan's gift off even to wash her hands.

"Charley is the best," Casey said, sitting down again. She smiled wryly at Stephanie. "This weekend was just what I needed." Her expression grew thoughtful. "A big stretch of time with him. It's the first vacation we've had together since we got engaged. And now"—Casey blushed—"I'm even more sure that marrying Charley's the right thing."

"You look like it is," Stephanie said. "You seem like you're very much in love."

Casey blinked. "Yeah, I guess I do. You're noticing stuff like that more these days."

Stephanie wrinkled her forehead. "I guess I do because of Jonathan."

Casey's gaze traveled to Stephanie's hand. "That's new," she commented, pointing at the ring.

"Just a friendship ring," Stephanie said quickly, but she was glad Casey had noticed.

"From Jonathan?"

Stephanie pretended to act shocked. "Who else? I don't give away my friendship to just anyone."

"I take it you spent some time together this weekend," Casey said with a smile.

"We did." Stephanie paused, then laughed. "And not just working." She filled Casey in on all their dates.

Casey pulled on her nightshirt and eyed Stephanie. "Are you guys getting serious?"

"Serious?" Stephanie's stomach flip-flopped at the word. "Uh, no. Not *serious* serious. But . . ." She couldn't go on. To herself she added, serious enough for now.

"Stephanie, I think you're falling in love with him."

Stephanie wanted to deny it but couldn't. "I think I am."

Casey's jaw dropped, then she closed her mouth, and Stephanie could see she looked embarrassed.

"I know," Stephanie said quickly. "It's all pretty fast, but I've never met anyone like him. I think this might be the real thing. Not that we're close to getting engaged or anything like you and Charley."

Casey looked at Stephanie, amazed. Her mouth widened into a great big smile. "Stephanie Keats, I never thought I'd see you like this. You're glowing. You're really in love!"

Stephanie's palms went sweaty, and she shot back, "I know, that's what scares me!"

Tuesday morning, Nancy cornered Jake just before the weekly *Wilder Times* editorial meeting. The newspaper office was chaotic, with everyone talking about the weekend.

But the meeting was the furthest thought from Nancy's mind. She had some really happy news and wanted to tell Jake.

"So what's up?" he asked as she pulled him aside.

"Bess," she said. "I just talked to her on the phone. She's decided to come back to school, Jake. And soon."

Jake's whole face lit up. "Hey, that's the best news, Nancy. What changed her mind?"

"George and Ned. But Ned mostly," Nancy said. "Whatever he said made an impression on her. He managed to get through to her when no one else could."

"Good," Jake said. "The hero riding up on the white charger to save the day."

"Jake!" Nancy exclaimed, confused by Jake's mild sarcasm.

"Just kidding," Jake said, squeezing her hand. "He's a great guy, and I'm happy for Bess."

"I really miss her." Nancy hesitated a moment. "And I sort of miss you, too."

"Me?" Jake looked shocked.

"What I mean is, I wasn't very together this weekend, and I'm sorry I kind of laid all my problems on you."

Jake brushed her hair off her face and shook his head. "I don't feel like you've laid all your problems on me. I'm just worried about you. You left home angry."

Nancy's jaw tightened. "Yeah, well, I'll have to deal with that, but"—she put her hand up to stop Jake before he could interrupt—"in my own way, in my own time."

Jake threw his hands up. "Whatever works for you, Nancy," he said evenly, but Nancy read the confusion in his face.

He still didn't get it. He thought a phone call home to her dad and Avery would solve everything.

"As long as *I* still work for you," he added, breaking into her silence.

Nancy looked up quickly. "Oh, Jake. Hey, this has nothing to do with you. You and I work just fine together," she hurried to assure him. But even as she pulled him close for a kiss, she wasn't sure that was absolutely true.

A few minutes later they went back to the editorial meeting, which was just starting, and grabbed the last two seats at the conference table.

Nancy couldn't immediately focus on what the editor-in-chief, Gail Gardeski, was saying. Nancy was still heady from her conversation with Bess. She felt so grateful to Ned for bringing Bess around. Leave it to Ned. He had a steady calm about him that made people want to confide in him. And he never judged anyone or anything. No, Nancy wasn't surprised about Ned. In fact, she felt so good about it, she decided she'd call him later and thank him.

Jake's voice caught her attention. He was telling the staff something about the counterfeit tape scam they'd stumbled into over the weekend. "I think I could work up a really interesting article about the damage this sort of thing does in the recording industry. Prick students' consciences a bit. When they buy pirated albums they're cheating the musicians and artists out of their fair share of the take."

"Run with it," Gail said. "I like the idea. What happened to the people involved?" she asked. "The Wilder connection?"

"Lily was arrested," Nancy informed Gail. "But I just found out today that Jeff Rayburn had already turned himself in to the police Monday morning. Kate Terrell talked him into it. The court might cut him some slack because he came clean. He could end up with community service instead of jail time."

"Maybe I can work that into the piece," Jake said. Nancy listened to Jake discuss how he could fill in the background of his story. He sounded so smart and savvy when he talked about his articles. But in spite of all his reporter instincts, he was sometimes a bit dense. Or he had been this weekend. Why couldn't Jake understand her feelings?

Ned had. Right away. With hardly any explanation on her part. Her home life until then had been just her and her dad, with Hannah in the background. Now everything had changed. Maybe it was natural, as Jake said, but that didn't mean she shouldn't feel upset. Or that she had to be thrilled about Avery's taking over her home.

Jake's touch on her wrist transported her back to the present. He was still talking to the staff and Gail, but when he caught her eye, she felt an incredible feeling of warmth shoot from her toes to the top of her head. For a second she couldn't catch her breath, and all thoughts of Avery and her dad flew right out of her mind.

Only Jake made her feel like this. She was just expecting too much from him. Jake had known her for a couple of months, Ned for years.

Jake wasn't a mind reader. But he was her guy. Nancy curled her fingers in his and couldn't wait for the meeting to end, so they could go off somewhere and be alone together. Yes, it was good to be back *home* at Wilder.

In her room in Jamison Hall, George sat at her desk, going through the mail she'd received while she was away. She read a letter from the Student Loan Office one more time. The office had contracted with a loan-servicing center to handle the bursar bills of any students who were interested. George folded the letter and stared out her window. It sounded like a good idea. She'd talk to Will about it soon to see what he thought.

"Did you get one of those letters, too?"

George looked up as her roommate, Pam Miller, came into the room. She grinned. "What's doing, Pam?"

"Not much. It's been kind of fun, if quiet, here

this weekend with you gone." Pam poked George playfully, then tapped the letter in George's hand. "Eileen O'Connor and I got one of these, too," she said. "We talked about it. We're both thinking of signing on. How about you?"

"Sounds good to me," George said. "I was just thinking of phoning the information number in the letter to get more details."

"Good idea," Pam said, tossing her stuff onto the bed. "Let me know what you find out. I've got to get to class now."

George reached for the phone, but before she could pick it up, it rang.

"George?"

"Bess? You okay?"

"I'm fine, George, really." And George knew that was true. Bess's voice sounded—well—more like Bess again.

"Did Nancy tell you the big news?"

"No. I haven't seen her today, Bess."

"Oh, well, I'm coming back to Wilder, George."

"All right!" George shouted into the phone and jumped up. "I am so happy." She caught Pam's eye and mouthed that Bess would be back. Pam gave a silent cheer, then grabbed some books and left.

"What changed your mind?" George asked.

Bess told her about her discussion with Ned. "But it was talking to you, too."

"I was afraid for a while I might have made things worse that day when I came over."

184

"No way," Bess asserted. "You sort of opened the door. I really began to think more clearly after you left. But, in the end, I guess I changed my own mind about stuff. Myself. Paul—" George heard Bess falter over the name. "Paul," she resumed in a steady voice. "It will still be hard to get over Paul and the accident. But he wasn't the only person I loved at Wilder. I have so many friends I care about, and George . . ." Bess gave a small laugh. "Can you imagine your college experience without me?"

George laughed. "No. I wouldn't even begin to try. But when, Bess? When will you be back?"

"Next week. Maybe."

"Next week?" George was ecstatic.

"I go to the doctor for a checkup tomorrow, but on the phone he said he thought I'm almost as good as new. I'll still have my cast, but in a few more weeks that'll be off."

"Bess Marvin, you're beginning to sound like your old self again," George said happily.

"Yeah." On the other end of the line Bess paused. "Hey, coz—thanks for being there for me."

"You bet. So, anything you want me to pass on to Leslie?"

Bess chuckled on the other end of the phone. "Tell her that her days and nights of a nice, neat, orderly room are almost over."

"She'll love that."

"Tell her I miss her, too, okay?" Bess added,

a catch in her voice. "You won't believe it, but it's true."

"I believe it, I believe it." George paused, then said, her eyes misting over, "It's good to have you back."

"Wrong tense, George—I'm not there yet."

Right tense, George thought. Bess was already coming back in many ways that counted. And George was sure she'd be even better after she got to Wilder.

But to Bess, George said, "Right. So get moving. Wilder is definitely not wild enough without you."

NEXT iN NANCY DREW ON CAMPUS™:

Bess has returned to Wilder, but she's far from her old self. Behind her brave smile, the tragic accident is still taking a secret toll. And while Bess is back on campus, George may be gone soon. Her tuition money has vanished in a scam, and if Nancy can't get to the bottom of it, George will have no choice but to drop out of school! Jonathan, meanwhile, has come out and said the words Stephanie has longed to hear: "I love you." So why is she suddenly flirting with every guy she meets? Nancy, however, is just flirting with trouble. As good as things are with Jake, she's met someone who's brought back memories of the good old days with Ned Nickerson . . . in *New Beginnings*, Nancy Drew on Campus #17.